---

about the authors

ALFRED DE MUSSET (1810–1857) was a French poet, play-wright, and novelist. He was born in Paris to a well-off family and turned to writing after first studying to be a doctor. Influenced by Lord Byron and Shakespeare, he typified the Romantic movement, not least in his passionate liaison with the bisexual authoress George Sand, who inspired *Gamiani*. He died in 1857 of a heart malfunction.

JOHN BAXTER's books include biographies of Federico Fellini, Luis Buñuel, Woody Allen, Stanley Kubrick, and Robert De Niro, and the memoir *We'll Always Have Paris: Sex and Love in the City of Light*. Born in Australia, he lives in Paris.

GAMIANI,

or

TWO NIGHTS

of EXCESS

GAMIANI,

or

TWO NIGHTS *of* EXCESS

alfred de musset

{ *a naughty french novel* }

translated by john baxter

HARPER ● PERENNIAL

NEW YORK ● LONDON ● TORONTO ● SYDNEY

HARPER ● PERENNIAL

FIRST HARPER PERENNIAL EDITION PUBLISHED 2007.

Designed by Joy O'Meara

Library of Congress Cataloging-in-Publication Data is available upon request.

ISBN: 978-0-06-123724-9
ISBN-10: 0-06-123724-8

07   08   09   10   11   ❖ /RRD   10   9   8   7   6   5   4   3   2   1

INTRODUCTION

a devil in the flesh

gamiani, or two nights of excess
by Baron de Alcide Mxxx, alias Alfred de Musset

by John Baxter

In 1833, the appearance in Paris of a cheaply produced, blisteringly erotic and sacrilegious novelette called *Gamiani, or Two Nights of Excess*, went largely unnoticed.

Supposedly the memoir of "Baron Alcide de Mxxx," it described how a young man-about-Paris, besotted with a mysterious but beautiful Italian countess named Gamiani, hides in her bedroom after a ball. From a wardrobe, he watches her introduce a virginal girl named Fanny to the pleasures of lesbian sex, until, aroused past endurance, he bursts out from his hiding place and joins them.

Though Gamiani chides him for his bad manners, she forgives his impetuosity and, while waiting for his ardor to revive, entertains her companions with stories of her own sexual initiation at the hands of a flagellating aunt and some depraved monks:

"A hidden door opened and a monk, clad in a costume like ours, approached me, mumbling some words. Then, drawing aside my dress, separating the skirt so that a piece fell on either side, he brought to light all the posterior quarter of my body.

"A slight quivering ran through the reverend brother. Doubtless roused to ecstasy by the sight of my flesh, his hand roved everywhere, halted for a moment upon my buttocks, finally found a resting place a little below them.

"'Tis by means of this place that a woman sins," intoned a sepulchral voice. "It is here she must suffer.'"

(Dominique Aury evidently had read *Gamiani* since, when she wrote *Histoire d'O* in the 1950s as Pauline Réage, she borrowed not only the gown Gamiani is forced to wear—black, high-collared, ankle-length, split down the back—but the quasi-religiosity of the torturers.)

After this, Gamiani, Alcide and Fanny alternate stories, competing to recall more and more flamboyant adventures: masturbation and group sex; bestiality with a donkey and an orang-utan; baths in fresh blood; a baroque orgy with an order of nuns (perhaps the legendary Sisters of Perpetual Indulgence?) who summon up Satan and a regiment of imps to satisfy their lusts.

Nobody faulted the comprehensiveness of *Gamiani*. Few major perversions were neglected, while some may have taken even seasoned sensualists by surprise. As a catalogue of depravity, it rivaled *Justine* and *The 120 Days of Sodom*, which had earned the Marquis de Sade imprisonment in the Bastille and the madhouse at Charenton.

Gamiani even ends on a nihilistic Sadeian note. The Countess poisons Fanny, then swallows a dose herself. It is, she explains in her dying breath, a gesture not of despair but of lust carried to the ultimate: "I, who have known every sensual extravagance, wished to discover whether in poison's death-grip . . . in this girl's last agony confounded with my own . . . there might not be a possibility . . . a possibility of pleasure . . . the extreme of pleasure in the extreme of pain."

Though the publication of erotica has always thrived in France, 1833 was an odd moment for a book like *Gamiani* to appear. Northern Europe basked in an era of Romance. Byron, Shelley and Keats had been dead for about ten years and Beethoven for five, but their influence was undiminished. And no writer embodied that spirit more completely than poet and novelist Louis Charles Alfred de Musset.

At twenty three, Musset was handsome, and, even in the full beard and mustache of the time, soft-featured and dreamy. An air of weary sensitivity was accentuated by a taste for pink suits and by his pallor, a symptom of the hereditary heart ailment that would kill him at forty-seven.

Imminent death haunted the young poet. "I cannot help it," he wrote. "In spite of myself, infinity torments me." It drove him to sample all the physical sensations. He smoked opium, and translated into French Thomas De Quincey's *Confessions of an English Opium-Eater*. A heavy drinker, he favored absinthe, the liqueur flavored with wormwood and known as "The Green Fairy," since a dash of water turns it greenly opalescent. Absinthe was credited with inducing creative fantasies, but could also lull the user into a semipermanent stupor.

Like John Keats, another poet who died before his time, Musset felt himself "half in love with easeful death." In the same year as *Gamiani*, he composed *Rolla*, a long poem in the style of Byron about a young sensualist, Jacques Rolla, who lavished the last of his fortune on one night with a luscious courtesan, then killed himself. In 1878, it would inspire Henrí Gervex to paint one of the most famous of all erotic canvases, showing Rolla taking one last lingering look at the girl sprawled nude and asleep in his bed before leaping out the window.

Musset knew many such stories, since he patronized Paris's better brothels, the *maisons closes*. Their whores were beautiful, the furnishings sumptuous, and every taste was catered to. Some rooms provided peepholes for voyeurs; some were fitted out as torture chambers. Others were furnished in Arab, Asian, even Eskimo style, complete with igloo. Painted backdrops depicted the desert or jungle, while the brothels' wardrobes contained costumes of all sorts: crinolines, military uniforms, nuns' habits.

Just when Musset felt he'd sampled everything, he met Amandine Aurore Lucie Dupin, Baroness Dudevant, who preferred the male name George Sand. Even in bohemian Paris, Sand created a sensation. Not only did she affect trousers, top hats and heavy boots, and smoke cigars, she also carried on flagrant affairs with both men and women.

Musset stammered his love in a series of passionate let-
ters. Always drawn to brilliant but doomed young artists—
her most famous lover was the tubercular Frédéric
Chopin—Sand accepted his invitation to a holiday in
Venice. It's doubtful they ever did more than share a gon-
dola, however, since he immediately fell ill, and Sand
started an affair with his doctor, leaving a crestfallen Musset to slink back to Paris alone.

It's against this background that Musset composed
Gamiani. The book was published just before his Venice
visit with Sand, but he modeled the bisexual countess on
her—for a time, many thought she helped write the
book—while echoes of Paris's absinthe bars, opium dens
and whorehouses pepper the text.

Surprisingly, few noticed the literary and intellectual su-
periority of *Gamiani*. It avoids the cliché terminology of
hack erotica, and also its phallocentricity. Alcide is the
weakest of the trio, while Gamiani is a liberated sexual
heroine, well ahead of her time.

> *"Tell me, what is a man, a lover, in comparison with me? Two
> or three bouts and he is done, overthrown. The fourth, and he
> gasps his impotence and his loins buckle. Pitiful thing! I remain
> strong, trembling, I remain unappeased. I personify the ardent
> joys of matter, the burning joys of the flesh. Luxurious, lewd,
> implacable, I give unending pleasure, I am love itself, love that
> slays!"*

It also achieves anatomical truth without dispelling the

erotic atmosphere, as in Gamiani's description of cunnilingus with a lingually gifted nun.

> *"In an instant, my head was gripped between my wrestling-companion's thighs. I divined her desires. Inspired by lust, I fell to gnawing upon her most sensitive parts. But I ill complied with her wishes. Quickly, she eluded me, slid out from under my body and, suddenly spreading my own thighs, immediately attacked me with her mouth. Her pointed, nervous tongue stabbed at me. Her teeth closed upon me and seemed about to tear me. . . . Then she let go: she touched me softly, injected saliva into me, licked me slowly, or mildly nipped my hairs and flesh with a refinement so delicate and at the same time so sensual that the very thought of it makes me come this minute with pleasure."*

Despite the obviousness of his pseudonym, Musset successfully hid his role as the author of *Gamiani*—wisely, since its anticlerical element alone could have led to prison.

To avoid the same fate, its anonymous publisher claimed to be based in Brussels. (Paris pornographers routinely gave their address as Constantinople, Athens, London, Benares, even Moscow, while opposite numbers in those locations claimed their books were "Published in Paris.") To cover his tracks further, he dispensed with nosy typesetters and reproduced the handwritten text and its illustrations in the lithographic technique used for drawings and posters.

Musset died in 1857 without ever acknowledging *Gami-*

ani, and though an 1864 edition carried an introduction supposedly written by him, the book was not definitively identified as his work until the 1990s.

Why did an author of his reputation compose this sulphurous fantasy? Obviously not for money, since it appeared in a tiny edition, nor for fame, since it was anonymous. Perhaps, despairing of ever possessing George Sand, and tormented by approaching death, Musset grasped his one chance to consummate his passion for her, if only in imagination.

He might also have wished to demonstrate once again his contempt for an implacable fate. At the moment in 1934, almost exactly a century after *Gamiani,* when *Tropic of Cancer* was published, and Henry Miller, another enthusiastic client of Paris's bars and brothels, spieled his Rabelaisian rant of bohemian life in the French capital as "a gob of spit in the face of Art, a kick in the pants to God, Man, Destiny, Time, Love, Beauty," somewhere, Alfred de Musset, alias "Count Alcide de Mxxx," may have raised a glass of absinthe in fraternal understanding.

GAMIANI,

or

TWO NIGHTS

of EXCESS

the first night

although midnight had come and gone, light still blazed in the tall windows of the Countess Gamiani's mansion, and the orchestra played on.

Minuet followed quadrille as the guests at her ball whirled and bowed, curtsied and spun, the gowns of the women swirling, their jewels glittering.

With the grace of an empress, the Countess, raven hair agleam, ivory pallor enhanced by the candles' golden light, basked in the success of the event. Joining the dancers only occasionally, she circulated tirelessly among those of her guests too aged, dignified or exhausted to do more than watch from the sidelines or graze on the buffets laden with exotic delicacies and the best of wines.

From time to time, some flushed young man accosted her to stammer a compliment. I joined the chorus of praise, although remaining, as always, silent and watchful, the detached observer. My comments, carefully considered and expressed, were, I believe and hope, appropriate to a woman of the Countess's quality, and betrayed nothing of the passion she aroused in me, while, for her part, Gamiani's manner retained the aloofness which was swiftly driving me out of my mind.

"You are most amiable, Monsieur Alcide," she murmured in response to my most recent remark.

To my besotted ear, the accent of her native Italy only complemented her pronunciation—the sure sign in a Frenchman that lust has overpowered reason.

"Your presence at my little soirée"—a wave of her hand managed to indicate the prodigality of her largesse and at the same time dismiss it as the merest vanity—"is sure proof that the evening has succeeded."

"Countess . . .," I began, "my dear, *dear* Gamiani . . ."

An amorous confession trembled on my lips, but I had no chance to express it.

"Ah," she said, looking over my shoulder. "The Comtesse de Vigny craves your attention. Don't let me deprive you of her company, my dear M. Alcide."

And before I could say more, she had moved on.

Watching her circulate through the crowded salon, I could only be struck even more by her grace, her good manners, her effortless style.

And yet . . . who *was* she, this so-called "woman of the world"? Everything about her was contradictory. Why, though young and beautiful, did she possess no husband, no lover (at least that I could discover), no close friends—not even any of those indigent relatives whom the warmth of wealth attracts as the lamp lures a moth? In the twelve months since she had launched herself in Parisian society, not a single cousin or niece had appeared, though a dozen could have lodged in her majestic residence without advertising their presence.

Each discovery about her uncovered another mystery. She was immensely wealthy, of course—but from what source? No vineyards, mines, banks, ships or estates bore the Gamiani name. As to her parentage, on learning she was of Italian descent, the most assiduous genealogists threw up their hands. In the inflaming heat of that mercurial nation, who knew what illicit liaisons might fester, even within the oldest families, or what resulting secrets would then lie walled up in the cloisters of its convents and monasteries?

She inspired rumors, not all of them benign. Even the most lavish praise for Gamiani's beauty, wit and good taste could terminate in a trickle of bile. Some blamed her inaccessibility on a heart as chill and hard as the diamonds she wore. Others suggested the reverse—a spirit too passionate, too romantic, which, profoundly wounded in some affair of the heart, had recoiled into solitude.

If I could probe beneath that surface, what motive might I find for her coldness toward me? Giving free rein to my facility for logic, I fantasized myself into the character of a psychic physician, surgically exposing her soul, dissecting it with the scalpel of my rationality.

But just as it seemed I had discounted every diagnosis, a voice from behind me proposed one which I had not considered.

"Ugh! I simply *detest* lesbians."

Startled, I turned to stare at the speaker. Gray-haired, thin-faced and sour, known to *tout Paris* as a relentless seducer of housemaids and a habitué of the less discriminating *maisons closes*, he was, all the same, not ignorant in these matters.

Gamiani a *lesbian!* How strangely the word "lesbian" rang in the ear. What images it summoned up: of voluptuous pleasures, of lusts carried to the ultimate degree, of endless foreplay, of releases which, once achieved, led only to greater but even less achievable delights.

Vainly, I tried to regain my former detachment, but in vain. I could think only of the Countess nude in the arms of another woman, hair tousled, body trembling; panting, gleaming with sweat, briefly spent, yet unsatiated, and whimpering for more . . .

Dizzy and sick, I pushed blindly through the crowd until I found an unoccupied side room, and collapsed, near to fainting, on a couch.

In time, I regained my detachment—and with it a determination the force of which both astonished and excited me.

If the object of my desire indeed found her pleasure in the arms of other women, then I would observe her in the enjoyment of it—and, in watching, satisfy the lust that filled me.

Faintly, I became aware that the orchestra was no longer playing. Another sound had taken the place of music: the pattering of rain on the window.

Looking down on the courtyard, I saw lamplit cobbles swept by a shower. Under the portico, people were taking their leave. From the *vestiare*, relays of servants ferried hats, cloaks and canes, while others, holding umbrellas, sheltered departing guests to the carriages drawing up on the boulevard.

Everyone was too busy to notice me as I moved without haste toward the private apartments of the Countess.

Her rooms were all that I had expected in luxury and good taste, or could have hoped for in potential for concealment. Her parlor was furnished with gilded furniture so fragile it seemed scarcely capable of supporting its own weight, let alone a human body. Crossing the room, I slipped into her boudoir, to find a bed which, in contrast to the delicacy of the furniture in her salon, displayed an almost voluptuous excess. Opulent enough for some caliph or maharajah, it was enclosed by a mahogany canopy, the four pillars intricately carved with reliefs of oriental depravity. Curtains of rose damask were drawn back, to expose silk sheets, folded down on a feather mattress, plump and white.

On the far side of the room, a mirrored door stood ajar. It opened on a space somewhere in size between a large closet and a small dressing room. Gowns hung from a rail at the back. Slipping behind these, I sequestered myself in the farthest corner, content to remain there for as long as might be needed to observe the demon sabbath my fevered mind anticipated.

I know not how much time elapsed before I heard the

Countess enter the room. Concerned she might come straight to my hiding place, I burrowed deeper, listening to that rustle which signals only one action—a woman undressing.

By the time it became clear she would not be troubling me, I had moved to the partly open door, the better to observe the object of my desires and fantasies.

I did so just in time to see her pull tight the sash of a peignoir of midnight blue silk, slip her feet into black slippers and take a seat before the mirror of her dressing table. Standing behind her, her maid began unpinning her hair, which cascaded down over her shoulders in a sable flood.

From my coign of vantage, I appraised the maid: plump and blonde, with the kind of body that invited fantasy. Was she to be the Countess's partner in her debauch?

Apparently not, since Gamiani said, "Julie, I won't need you any more tonight. You can go to bed."

But my disappointment turned to anticipation when she continued, "And if you hear sounds from my bedroom, don't be worried. On no account should I be disturbed."

"Yes, *madame la comtesse.*"

Confident now that I would not be thwarted in my desire, and congratulating myself on my audacity, I ventured even farther from the shelter of the hanging gowns, the better to observe.

By then, the Countess had left the bedroom for her parlour. From there, I heard a voice I didn't recognize.

"It's *so* inconvenient," said the newcomer in a voice too

cultured to be that of the maid. "Pouring with rain, and no carriage."

"It's just as distressing to me, dear Fanny," replied Gamiani. "I'd send you home in my own carriage—but just today, my coachman took it to the harness makers."

Fanny? Mentally, I reviewed the night's guests. Did I remember a girl named Fanny?

Wait . . .

Wasn't that the name of the Pleyel girl? I'd seen the Countess chatting with her during the evening; short curly black hair, slim but full-breasted, with enormous eyes that betrayed her mother's Russian ancestry. But surely she was still a child; no more than fifteen years of age?

But if this was Gamiani's choice of partner, I would be lying if I didn't admit that the vision of them together inflamed my desire even further. With blood pounding in my ears, I only half listened to their conversation.

"My mother will be worried . . . ," said the girl.

"Don't worry, dear. I've sent someone to tell her you'll be spending the night here."

"You're too kind. I hate to put you to this trouble."

"What trouble? It will be a delight. A little . . . adventure. And don't worry that I'll exile you to some cold bedroom either. You'll sleep here with me."

The girl's voice betrayed surprise, nervousness and a hint of something else—anticipation? Desire?

"But . . . with both of us in the same bed," she said. "Well, you won't get a minute's sleep."

In any affair, there are moments when the matter is decided, and what follows, even if unacknowledged, becomes inevitable. As, in the silence after Fanny's unconsidered remark, I apprehended, with a lurch of my heart, that everything I had wished for this evening was about to occur, it became clear to me that Fanny and Gamiani, consciously or not, shared the same realization. Sleep was the last thing on the mind of either.

Excitement made the dressing room, already stuffy with clothes, even more claustrophobic. Unable any longer to suppress the thrusting of my erect flesh, I unbuttoned myself to release it—then, in a reckless frenzy of lust, threw off the rest of my clothes, to stand naked, my skin, like that of some invisible voyeur set free in a fashionable soiree, deliciously caressed on every side by scented velours and silks.

A moment later, the Countess and her companion reentered her bedroom, and I saw that I had been right. The girl was indeed Fanny de Pleyel, short-haired doe-eyed granddaughter of the eminent academician Aristide de Pleyel, a tender innocent attending her first "grown-up" soirée.

Apparently she remained a little doubtful about the sleeping arrangements, since the Countess took her hand reassuringly.

"At boarding school, didn't you ever share your bed with a friend?"

"Well . . . yes . . .," said the girl doubtfully.

"Then let you and I be like two friends; two schoolgirls."

Drawing the girl toward her, the Countess tilted her face upward, and softly kissed her lips.

Fanny's blush flowed across her cheeks, down her throat and across the slopes of her breasts revealed in her deep *décolleté*. But she didn't resist.

"I sent my maid to bed," continued Gamiani. "But we can do very well without her. I'll help you undress."

Reaching behind the girl, she released, one by one, the hooks and eyes that held her dress together. Fanny, eyes downcast, didn't resist, even when the silk gown slipped to the floor around her feet.

Fortunately, she had not yet succumbed to the fashion for a full corset, so her light bustier was easily unlaced. Without a pause, the Countess lifted it away from her body. Before the girl could protest—though she showed no sign of wishing to do so—a twitch of shoulder tapes released her slip and it too dropped, leaving her, except for her gartered stockings and shoes, quite nude.

"How beautifully you're made, my dear," said the Countess. "You have a marvelous body."

I could only agree. Fanny displayed at the same time the innocence of youth and its boldness. Her high, firm, pointed breasts might never have known a lover's touch, yet their erect nipples showed an eagerness for it. Her mouth seemed made for kisses, while her secret places, veiled in little more than a mist of hair, were meltingly ready for a caressing tongue, and for even more ardent attentions. As for her white skin, I must confess that I longed to see it hatched with the livid weals of a thrashing.

As if to confirm this perception of her true nature, Fanny didn't shrink from Gamiani's appraising gaze, nor try to cover herself. Instead she looked up at the Countess and smiled.

"You find my body . . . agreeable?"

"Ravishing." Gamiani took a step back, the better to appraise her marble purity. "Such whiteness! I'm jealous."

"You're just saying that to flatter me. You yourself are far more beautiful."

What boldness! What calculation! In less than a minute, this apparent innocent had metamorphosed into an accomplished coquette.

But she was foolish to provoke a seducer as skilled as Gamiani, who, though barely older in years, was many more times her superior in the strategies of the boudoir.

"Me more beautiful?" said Gamiani, falsely naïve. "How sweet of you to say so, my child. But this is a matter easily settled. . . ."

Tugging free the sash of her peignoir, she let the garment ripple to the carpet, revealing herself completely naked.

" . . .once we are on level ground."

I gasped so loudly that the women would surely have heard had they not been preoccupied in mutual admiration. It was all I could do not to clutch my erect manhood and spend my seed simply at the sight of them.

Startled by the frankness of Gamiani's gesture, Fanny stepped backwards. Catching a heel in the clothing still pooled around her feet, she would have fallen had the Countess not grasped her wrist.

"Why the confusion?" she inquired. "You would think

you were in the presence of a gentleman, and not just"— she smiled—"your little friend from boarding school."

Swiveling the girl and placing an arm around her shoulders, she indicated the large *verre chéval* on the other side of the room. The long mirror in its mahogany frame enclosed the reflection of their nude bodies as perfectly as in a canvas by Madame Vigée Le Brun.

"Look, now," said Gamiani. "If this were indeed the Judgment of Paris, and he charged with presenting his apple to the more beautiful of us, whom do you think he would choose?"

Had I been that Paris, son of Priam, lover of Helen, the luckless authority called on to decide which of the three goddesses, Hera, Athena and Aphrodite, was the most lovely, I would have pondered long, and probably unavailingly, on the rival merits of Gamiani and Fanny Pleyel.

Seeing them naked together was to see a flower both in its first form, as a barely open bud, and in the richness of maturity. Where Fanny's breasts were bold and tight, those of Gamiani drooped softly, roundly, their nipples red and swollen as ripe strawberries, while the lips of her *sexe*, unlike Fanny's discreet fold, pouted moist and pink within a nest of curling black hair.

With her free hand, Gamiani palmed Fanny's breast, weighing it, her thumb gently toying with the nipple, which sprang boldly erect.

"Ah," said the Countess in satisfaction, "look how she smiles to see herself so lovely . . . and indeed you deserve a kiss on the forehead, on your cheeks, upon your lips . . ."

Unable any longer to contain herself, Gamiani fitted the deed to her words and let her mouth, lascivious and ardent, stray over Fanny's body.

"She is beautiful everywhere, everywhere . . .," she muttered in an ecstasy of lust.

Disconcerted, trembling, the girl did nothing to oppose her—until, catching sight of their reflection in the mirror, she seemed to realize for the first time that what had appeared a moment before like the most chaste of classical images was now within a hair's breadth of flagrant pornography.

"Oh, what are you doing?" She writhed in Gamiani's grasp. "Please, madame, I beseech you. . . ."

Impatiently, the Countess swept Fanny into her arms, strode to the bed and threw the girl down onto it, like a beast which, having overmastered its prey, made ready to tear it apart.

Half embedded in the soft mattress, Fanny, one hand raised as if to shield her face, stared, wide-eyed, at the panting, flushed Gamiani.

"Madame, please . . . you frighten me . . . I'll scream. . . ."

A quick smile passed across the lips of the Countess. She knew, as did I, that no cry from the bedroom would be heeded tonight.

Gamiani lunged forward, stretching her body over that of the trembling Fanny. Grasping the hands which the girl raised in protest, she thrust them firmly into the pillow above her head, while her body easily suppressed her efforts to writhe out from beneath her.

"Fanny, stop! You'll see . . . I will give you such pleasure. . . ."

"This is wicked," protested the girl. "It's wrong."

But, as Fanny was now discovering, the body knows certain things that the mind will not acknowledge. For all her protests, a new and lascivious feeling was flooding through her, a lust to which she longed to abandon herself.

Gamiani felt it too, and redoubled her efforts, knowing they would soon achieve success.

"Ah, how you tremble, child!" she murmured, herself half drunk with pleasure. "Yes, squeeze me, my little one, my love."

Her mouth grazed the ears, the closed eyes and gaping lips of the now helpless Fanny.

"Squeeze tight! Tighter still!"

"No!" protested the girl. "You're killing me. . . ."

"How beautiful you are in your pleasure! How you enjoy it. . . . Oh God."

This pious outburst, in an instant during which Gamiani's body arched back from that of her lover, her eyes closed and she whimpered deep in her throat, signaled, I realized later, the first of the night's numerous climaxes.

Slithering down the bed, the beautiful Italian wrenched apart the girl's thighs and buried her face between them. Fanny resisted, but only until some cunning flick of the tongue tripped that catch which unlocks a woman's body to the invasion of pleasure. With a sob, Fanny raised her knees, spread them wide, and reached down to plunge her fingers into Gamiani's luxuriant hair.

The events I observed breathlessly for the next hour will remain forever in my memory. What looked like rape was, I quickly understood, a kind of dance, in which resistance and the overcoming of it served to prolong and enhance pleasure. Each kiss gained, each nipple suckled or finger insinuated was thus a victory, and all the more richly to be relished.

As for Fanny, any innocence that survived her initiation quickly sublimed in the heat of their shared passion. Soon, it was she who sprawled across the body of Gamiani, contending for kisses, *her* tight curls that filled the spread thighs of the Countess, *her* tongue that extorted the release which Gamiani's body was all too ready to surrender.

Pleasure induced in the Countess a delirium of passion which recognized no limits. The appalling Donatien de Sade contended that torture and even murder were permissible in worship of the only God he recognized—that of the Self. Watching Fanny and the Countess, I became aware, for the first time in my young life, that indeed, for some people in the heat of lust, any act might appear permissible if it contributed to the gratification of the senses.

At last, Gamiani, sated, rolled off the recumbent Fanny. Leaving the girl sprawled on the bed, pale and exhausted, like a glorious corpse, she seated herself before her dressing table and, making a choice among the half dozen crystal flagons, cooled her brow and shoulders with *eau de cologne*.

Rested and refreshed, she rose and strolled the room naked, admiring herself in its mirrors, even that on the door of her closet. I shrank back into the darkness, but she had eyes only for herself.

She dragged her fingers through her knotted and sweaty hair, cupped her breasts to weigh them and observe them approvingly in her reflection, even slipped a finger into the now-swollen crevice between her thighs and, withdrawing it, first sniffed her juices, then tasted them.

This action revived her barely dormant lust. Slumping into a wide armchair that faced the bed, she hooked one leg over the arm.

"Fanny, darling. Watch me. . . ."

On the bed, Fanny sleepily turned her head and half opened her eyes.

Licking a forefinger, Gamiani laid it in the spread lips of her sex and began to tease herself to yet another climax.

Seeing her partner at her pleasure breathed on that glowing coal of lust which, having been ignited within Fanny, would never be extinguished. As if of its own volition, one hand strayed across her own belly while the other drifted to her breasts and toyed with her nipples.

The sight drove me entirely out of my mind.

One part of me wanted simply to declare my presence; to assert that other beings existed outside this hermetic universe of their creation. But another, more greedy, desired only to share their pleasure.

Yanking back the door of the closet, I stepped out. Naked, flaming, enpurpled, terrible, I crossed the room in a few strides and hurled myself onto the body of Fanny.

What did she think? Perhaps, at that point, she had

gone beyond thinking, and entered that realm of pure sensation where reality and fantasy fuse. Did she imagine me some devil or satyr, summoned up by the demonic skills of her seducer, or dredged from the depths of her own erotic imagination?

Either way, she made no resistance. Her thighs parted, and in an instant I was inside her, buried to the hilt between her thighs which, as I began my urgent strokes, responded to each movement with a motion no less eager. Her legs locked around my hips. Our tongues touched, burning, stinging; our souls melted and fused.

"Oh, my God!" she moaned. "They are *killing* me. . . ."

And in that instant, as I gushed inside her, I felt her spend too, seeming to dissolve under me; to indeed die— as has been said of this moment of pleasure—a little death.

"Get off her! Get away!"

Gamiani, no longer in her chair, knelt on the bed beside us, clawing and biting as she tried to wrest me from her friend.

Lifting my head, I found myself staring up into that face which, only an hour or two earlier, I had thought the most desirable in the universe. And now, even drained as I was, and briefly free of lust, that judgment was one I could not recant.

On impulse, I put my hands behind Gamiani's thighs and jerked her toward me, parting her legs at the same time, so that her moist sex lay invitingly close to my lips.

"Come nearer," I said urgently. "Steady yourself on your arms."

Audacity was once again rewarded. Gripped, as I'd hoped she would be, by the frenzy of the moment, and without a moment's hesitation, the lustful Countess toppled forward on her hands, creating an arch over the bodies of myself and Fanny—who, as my devouring tongue probed the most fiery crevices of Gamiani's body, reached up and—insensate, lost—caressed the breasts that swung ripely above her.

The double stimulation aroused Gamiani to unendurable ecstasy. Her entire body shook in a spasm so intense I feared for her life.

Letting her body fall heavily onto the bed, she lay on her back, panting, sweating, arms outstretched.

She took a deep, shuddering breath. "You've killed me."

Had I then bested this voracious and passionate woman? Had I definitely satisfied the creature whom I'd watched overwhelm the girl who lay now beneath me, as a bolting horse mows down the infant who's strayed into the road?

Such was my arrant male hubris—doomed, in the presence of women such as these, to survive no more than a few seconds.

As, at the thought of having achieved my desires with Gamiani, my manhood began to stir, Fanny too returned to life—and, not simply to life, but to lust.

"My darling," she murmured in my ear.

Arms that lightly rested around my neck now tightened, legs crept around my calves to clasp me even more tightly—if that were possible—than before.

"Come to me."

Her hips shifted beneath mine as, with minute movements and adjustments, she guided me within her once again.

"Shift a little . . . more . . . oh, yes . . . *there. . . .*"

Her movements became more urgent, her hips thrusting, driving me even deeper.

"Faster now! Yes! Go, go!"

Helpless to control myself, I gushed inside her for the second time as, at the same moment, her spasms announced she had also reached her climax.

"Oh, I feel it," she said in delight. "I'm *swimming. . . .*"

And we lingered there, I prone upon her, she beneath me, tense, motionless; our mouths, half-opened, were pressed together, softly exchanging our near-unto-dying breath.

Gradually we recovered control of ourselves. Rolling away from Fanny, I lay on my back between the two of them until, catching the eye of the Countess, I felt, as I sensed did she, the full absurdity of what had transpired.

Free now of the animal urges that had driven her, Gamiani sat up and, leaning back on the pillows, drew a sheet over her breasts. Fanny too crept under the covers, then, softly, began to weep, as will a child when it knows a sin has been committed but can do nothing but surrender to regret.

"Well, Monsieur Alcide," the Countess said dryly. "This has been a most unfortunate adventure, and a disagreeable surprise. I would never have suspected you of so cowardly an ambush. I blush to recall what took place here tonight."

Sitting on the edge of the bed—in part, I must admit, to obscure the signs of continuing lust which the presence of these two luscious creatures continued to excite—I hurried to defend myself; to declare finally my fatal, irreversible passion—a passion which the frost of Gamiani's manner had induced me to express in the only way open; in stealth and violence . . .

But Gamiani brushed this aside. The depth of my feeling was irrelevant, it seemed. Where I had transgressed was in the matter of good taste.

"Surely you realize, monsieur; no woman would ever pardon one who has discovered her . . ." She averted her eyes from the swell of Fanny's body under the sheet, which she had been absently caressing— "weakness."

"My dear Gamiani," I protested, "you can't for one moment believe that I would abuse a secret I owe more to chance than to my own temerity. No, it would be too ignoble. Never while I live will I forget the intense pleasures we have tasted—but be assured I will keep the recollection of them to myself."

Sensing that my sincerity was having some effect, I hurried on, "If I have acted wrongly, bear in mind that delirium sat enthroned in my heart."

Before she could respond, I addressed myself to Fanny, who, having stopped crying, now peeped, swollen-eyed, from beneath the sheets.

"Calm yourself, my dear. Shed tears over pleasure?

Never! Think only of the sweet sympathy which a short moment ago united us. If you prefer, believe it a dream; a dream that belongs only to you—because I swear I would never spoil my memory of our happiness by confiding it to others."

My sincerity appeared to have won them over—that, or the simple realization on their part that any damage to their reputations or mine was now well and truly done, and that all three of us must trust one another to keep our common secret. The knowledge made me bold—sufficiently so to take a chance at losing all I had achieved, or winning much more.

"Do we not rather owe it to ourselves," I said, "to preserve our memories of the delights we have known together—delights . . ."

Boldly, I laid one hand on the swell of Fanny's hip under the white silk and placed the other on the shoulder of Gamiani as she leaned back against her pillows.

" . . . we may know again."

Among connoisseurs of innuendo, no device is regarded with more respect than the raised eyebrow. Scorn and skepticism, complacency and amusement, suspicion and disdain . . . all lie within its purview.

The eyebrow which Gamiani raised to me appeared to encompass all of these—but as well some subtleties which, at the time, eluded me, but which, before our time together was over, would return to haunt all my days to come.

"How capricious you are, Alcide," she said at last. "Oh, all right . . . I forgive you." She patted the hand that rested on her shoulder. "You have understood that, for a creature as isolated from feeling as myself, pleasure is too rare to be wasted."

I moved to protest this estimate of herself, but she stopped me.

"Truly, you know nothing of me before I came here a year ago. You cannot know what took place . . . elsewhere . . . before. . . . And it is better, far better, that you do not."

Then, however, in an instant, her former lightness returned. Playfully, she twitched back the rest of the sheet, revealing a startled, blushing Fanny.

"So, my dear friends," said the Countess, "let us give ourselves over to joy . . . to voluptuousness; as if this were our last night among the living. . . ."

She held out her arms to Fanny. "Come! Fanny, kiss me then. Kiss me, mad creature! Let me bite you," she hissed. "Let me suck you. Let me inhale you to your bones' own marrow."

The girl needed no further invitation, but slithered up the body of her seducer. Their kiss, almost inhumanly prolonged, recalled to my fevered imagination another strain of the Gothic—its tales of those eldritch creatures, *vampyres*, which feed on the blood of their victims, leaving them living shells, inhabited only by the lust for yet more of their vile food.

But even as my spirit recoiled from such diseased fantasies, my body lusted to join in their fearful rites—as Gamiani was not slow to realize.

As Fanny let her head fall onto Gamiani's breast, like a baby who, briefly sated, slips from the nipple with sleepy eyes and open mouth, the Countess lazily raised her head from the pillow to regard me. Her eyes observed my manhood's engorged state.

"Oh, the superb animal! What wealth is here."

"You covet it, Gamiani?" I said. "Why, 'tis then for you."

I would have sprung forward then and quenched my lust in a single glorious thrust, had the Countess not held up her hand and, with the quick grimace and waggling finger of a schoolmistress, warned me off. The arrogance! I was in no mood to endure yet more of her regal disdain. I had been patient long enough, and the events of the evening had made me bold.

"You disdain this pleasure?" I said.

Leaping onto the bed, I scrambled to her on hands and knees until our faces were only inches apart. "You shall extol it once you have drunk deep of it."

Roused from her erotic daze, Fanny had rolled away. Gamiani sprawled beneath me, no longer the ravening predator but the helpless prey. I felt as a Roman general must have felt as, topping a hill at the head of his cohort, he looked down on a tranquil countryside, ripe for pillage.

"Remain lying down just as you are," I ordered.

For a moment, she seemed ready to resist, but I shoved her back onto the pillows.

Slapping her thighs, I indicated she should part them. "Advance the part I am to attack."

Sulkily, she did so, exposing in utter shamelessness the

crevice I had lusted to occupy. The sheer beauty of her body, all open to me at last, set me afire.

"Ah! What beauties!" I cried. "What a posture! Quick, Fanny! Wrap your legs around the Countess."

Without hesitation, the girl squirmed behind the Countess, locked her strong arms under her armpits and, wrapping her legs around her thighs, dug her heels into their soft flesh, forcing them even more widely open. Thus was the object of my lust presented to me as a prisoner, helpless to resist.

Resist Gamiani did, however, writhing and twisting in Fanny's grasp, though her struggles merely served to fan my ardor.

Taking my erect and enpurpled organ in hand, I plunged it, dagger-like, into her sweet wound.

Guide this terrible weapon, this fiery blade, I muttered in my fever to an all-but-insensate body, *Batter it against the breach. . . . Be steadfast there! . . . Too hard, too rapid . . . Gamiani . . . ah, you are making away with the emblem of pleasure.*

The Countess's agitation as I thrust into her resembled that of one possessed by devils—a condition not ameliorated, I can attest, by Fanny, who, herself inflamed by this tripartite coupling, leaned over Gamiani's shoulder and passionately kissed her.

In a fury, I thrust with all the force at my command. Fanny toppled back, with Gamiani on top of her, and in an instant I was presented with the dizzying sight of not one but two wet, open, inviting *sexes*, neither more or less beautiful than the other.

Thus it was that, having had Gamiani on Fanny's body, I now made a furious assault upon her own unguarded gate. In a trice I was through it; and we were all three overwhelmed, smitten down by pleasure.

For many minutes after, we lay in companionable silence, recuperating from our excesses, regaining our energies.

Had this been a Tuscan hillside or Provençal glade, I fantasized, someone would have recounted a tale—from their own experience, or perhaps some *galant* story of former times, plucked from Boccaccio or Aretino.

I said as much to Gamiani—who, to my surprise, responded only with a snort of contempt.

"What need have we of stories? We, who are scarcely more than fantasies ourselves; will-'o-the wisps who exist in this world only as the most fugitive of dreams; or nightmares, rather, in the troubled sleep of some lesser god."

"You are too melancholy," I said. "Too dark. There is light and joy in this world if only you choose to seek it out."

"For some, perhaps. But not I."

Drawing aside the sheet that covered her magnificent body, she looked down at herself not with pleasure but with a kind of contempt, even hatred.

"Be aware, my dear Alcide, that I have divorced myself from nature. I am no longer capable of feeling anything except that which is horrible, extravagant. . . . I pursue the impossible."

She grimaced, and, in that instant, appeared what I never thought she could appear—ugly.

"Ah, how frightful it is," she cried, "to be consumed, to be laid waste by deceptions, disappointments; always to desire, never to be satisfied. My imagination . . . *kills* me."

I hastened to protest. "This state you speak of, Gamiani, is perhaps only temporary. You overfeed yourself on tragic literature."

And indeed much of what she said would not have been out of place in the Gothic novels of the English writers Walpole and Mrs. Radcliffe—most of which took as their setting the castles and abbeys of Gamiani's native Italy. It had never occurred to me the source of her sick imaginings was not the fiction of torture, rape and murder but the reality.

"You would console me?" Her voice was bitter. "Then let me tell me the kind of story you asked for—though in this case, the tale is real. . . ."

gamiani's story

"*i was brought up in italy* by an aunt who had been early widowed. I had reached my fifteenth year knowing nothing of worldly affairs. I was aware of religion only for its terrors. I spent my life praying to Heaven that I might be spared Hell's torments.

"My aunt inspired those dreads in me, nor ever did she temper them with the least indication of tenderness. I knew no sweetness but what came to me during my sleeping hours. My days were passed in the sadness that burdens the nights of someone condemned to death.

"But sometimes, in the morning, my aunt would call me to her bed. At those times her glances were sweet, her words flattering. She would draw me to her breast, have me lie upon her thighs, and all of a sudden clutch me in convulsive embraces. At such times, she would twist, squirm, fling back her head and swoon with a burst of wild laughter.

"Appalled, I would contemplate her, immobile, and I would fancy she had been taken by an epilepsy.

"My aunt had for several days been speaking to me of the sufferings, of the tortures to be endured in order to purchase forgiveness for one's sins. As a consequence of a long discussion she had with a Franciscan, I was summoned to meet the reverend brother.

"'My daughter,' he announced, 'you are growing up. The tempting demon is already able to discern you. And you will soon sense his attacks. If you are not pure, chaste, his arrows will succeed in finding their mark in you; if you avoid what soils you and remain clean, you will also remain invulnerable. Our Savior redeemed the world through His agonies. Through sufferings, you too will expiate your sins. Prepare yourself to undergo the martyrdom of redemption. Ask God for the necessary strength and courage; this evening you will be put to the proof. . . . Go, now, go in peace, my child.'

"Terrified by his words, I left the monk. Once alone, I wanted to pray, to think on God, but I could see nothing but images of the punishment awaiting me.

"My aunt came in the middle of the night. She ordered me to strip naked, to wash from head to toe, and to put on a strange black dress, tight-fitting around the neck, ample below and entirely parted behind.

"She dressed in a similar garment, and we left the house by carriage.

"An hour later, I found myself in a vast room hung in black and lit by a single lamp suspended from the ceiling.

"In the middle of the room stood a *prie-dieu* surrounded by cushions.

"'Kneel down,' said my aunt. 'Prepare yourself through prayer, and with fortitude bear all the pain God could visit upon us.'

"I had no sooner obeyed her than a hidden door opened and a monk, clad in a costume like ours, approached me, mumbling some words. Then, drawing aside my dress, separating the skirt so that a piece fell on either side, he brought to light all the posterior quarter of my body.

"A slight quivering ran through the reverend brother. Doubtless roused to ecstasy by the sight of my flesh, his hand roved everywhere, halted for a moment upon my buttocks, finally found a resting place a little below them.

"'Tis by means of this place that a woman sins,' intoned a sepulchral voice. 'It is here she must suffer.'

"Immediately these words left his mouth I felt myself being beaten—whipped by knouts, by thongs tipped with iron points. I clutched at the monk, screaming: 'Spare me! Spare me, I cannot bear this torture! Kill me rather than do this! I beg you to pity me.'

"'Miserable coward,' my aunt exclaimed. 'Do you then need my example?'

"Whereupon she exposed herself, completely naked, spreading her thighs wide apart, raising them. A storm of blows hissed down upon her. The executioner worked away with perfect calm. Her thighs were quickly covered with blood.

"But my aunt seemed unshaken. 'Harder!' she shouted. 'Ah! Harder! Still harder!'

"The scene spellbound me, I felt distracted, possessed of more than natural courage. I cried that I was ready to suffer, no matter what.

"My aunt stood up at once and covered me with burning kisses, while the monk tied my hands above my head and blindfolded my eyes.

"What am I to tell you? My torture began again, now twice as terrible. Soon numbed by pain, I hung motionless, no longer able to feel anything. Through the whistling of the lash, I was confusedly aware of cries, outbursts, hands slapping flesh. There was also demented laughter, nervous, spasmodic, the precursor of erotic joy. Sometimes the voice of my aunt, hoarse from lust, would rise and dominate that weird harmony, that orgiastic concert, that bloody saturnalia.

"I later learned that the spectacle of my torture had served to awaken her desires. Each one of my strangled moans and sighs had provoked in her a spurt of pleasure.

"At length, my tormentor, in all probability simply exhausted, brought his work to an end. Still immobile, I was half-dead from terror, resigned to death. As my senses revived, however, I experienced an extraordinary itching sensation. My body shivered. It was afire.

"I agitated myself lubriciously, as if to satisfy an insatiable desire. All of a sudden, two twitching arms locked round me; something—I could not tell what, but hot and straining—butted my thighs, then penetrated me. I thought I was being rent in two. I uttered a terrible scream, instantly smothered by explosions of laughter. Two or three frightful thrusts managed to complete the introduction of the sturdy flail that was ruining me. My bleeding thighs were glued to those of my adversary; it seemed as if our flesh were melting and consolidating into one body. Every one of my veins was blood-swollen, my nerves strained to the last pitch. The vigorous rubbing to which I was exposed, and which was effected with incredible agility, heated me to such a point I thought I had received the touch of a red-hot iron.

"Straightway, I fell into an ecstasy. I saw myself come to Heaven. A viscous and burning essence inundated me, penetrated to my bones, titillated me to the marrow. . . . Oh, 'twas too much. . . . I melted, like fiery lava. . . . I felt a devouring, irrepressible fluid race within me. I provoked its ejaculation by means of furious motions and fell, utterly spent, into a depthless abyss of unheard-of joy."

At this point in the Countess's narrative, Fanny, who had been listening with even more attentiveness and astonishment, could no longer contain herself.

"What a picture!" She shivered, making her breasts quiver, and I realized that this confession, far from horrifying her, was feeding her lust. "You'll send the devil back into our flesh."

"Then listen well," the Countess continued. "That's not the end of it. . . . My voluptuousness in the aftermath of my flogging soon changed into an atrocious agony. A score of monks flung themselves headlong upon me; twenty frenzied cannibals who did everything but devour my helpless flesh. When they were satisfied, my brutalized body lay abandoned upon the cushions. My head lolled. My eyes saw nothing. I was like a corpse and, as if indeed lifeless, was borne away to my bed."

"What infamous cruelty!" I exclaimed.

"There is yet more. Restored to life, recovered from my injuries, I understood for the first time the horrible perversity of my aunt and her companions in debauchery. Only the sight of the most ferocious tortures could excite these creatures. I swore a moral hatred for them. In my despairing vengeance, I extended that hatred to include all men."

"Though not women?" I inquired.

"At first, to all human beings. But my temperament was ardent. I had strong appetites to satisfy. For a time, I could satisfy them myself, alone, without the intervention of any animate creature. It was not until later I was cured of masturbation, and this by the sage instruction I received from the girls at the Convent of Redemption. Their fatal science doomed me forever. . . . But that story is for another time."

Here sobs choked the Countess's faded voice. Caresses were unavailing. To create a diversion, I turned to Fanny.

"And now you, my lovely one. In one night, you've been initiated into a wealth of mysteries. Come now, tell us how you felt your first sensual pleasure."

Despite all that had taken place between us, Fanny blushed becomingly. "I! I shouldn't dare."

"You won't plead modesty surely?"

"After the Countess's story? But anything I might be able to say would seem insignificant."

"Don't believe it for a minute, sweet little enchantress," I said.

"Perhaps she needs some encouragement," purred Gamiani. She reached out a hand to caress the girl's pale body. "A kiss for you, my beloved? Two hundred of them, if it will take that many to win you over. And look at Alcide. . . ."

At this, she drew attention to the state of furious erection into which her tale of torment and rape had roused me.

"How amorous he is. Look there. For the moment it rests, unused, but in an instant . . ."

Fanny quailed in mock—at least I hope it was mock—terror at the prospect, but I needed little encouragement to put Gamiani's threat into practice.

"No, no, enough, Alcide!" protested Fanny, wriggling away from us. "I have no strength left. Spare me, I beg you. . . . How lustful you are, Gamiani. . . . Alcide, be off with you! Get up! . . . Oh . . ."

"In this battle, none is spared," I told her sternly. "Either submit, or give us *The Odyssey* of your maiden years."

"You force me to," she pouted.

"Indeed we do!"

"Oh, very well."

Propping herself on one elbow, for all the world like a schoolgirl recounting the details of her summer vacation, and utterly indifferent to the provocative effect of her naked breasts, or the livid heiroglyphs scored by finger-nails or teeth on the white skin of her shoulders and thighs, she launched into her tale.

fanny's story

"*i was, i swear to you,* a complete innocent until I reached fifteen. Never had my thoughts dwelled upon the difference between the sexes.

"I lived thus, unburdened by care and in undoubted happiness, until, one extremely warm day, being alone in the house, I felt a need to put myself at my ease.

"I undressed myself. Virtually nude, I stretched out upon a divan. . . . Oh! I am so ashamed of it. . . . I lay full length, I spread my thighs, and, all unwittingly, adopted the most indecent of attitudes.

"The material covering the divan was glossy. Its coolness caused a voluptuous rubbing all over my body. Ah, how freely I breathed! A sweetly penetrating atmosphere surrounded me. I was in a delicious ecstasy. It seemed to me as if a new life were flooding into my being, that I had become strong, that I was taller, that I was drawing a divine breath, that I was swooning into the rays of a superb sunset. . . ."

"But this is poetry!" I exclaimed.

"I am precisely describing my sensations," said Fanny reprovingly. "My eyes wandered complacently over my own person, my hands flew to my neck, to my breast; lower down, they halted, and, despite myself, I fell into a deep reverie. Examining myself, touching my body anew, I wondered whether all this might not have an end, a purpose.

"Words of love and of lovers repeatedly came to my mind, though their meaning remained inexplicable. Instinctively, I understood something was lacking in me. I could not define it, but I desired it with all my soul. My arms opened as if to seize the object of my yearnings. I went so far as to hug myself. I touched myself, caressed myself. So great was my need to have a body to grasp that I laid hands upon myself, thinking I was someone else, another person.

"Overcome, transported, I grasped a pillow, squeezed it between my thighs, took another into my arms and kissed it madly, enveloping it in passion. What pleasure. It seemed to me I was melting, that I was disintegrating. I cried aloud, 'Oh my God!' I was wet. Wet all over. Unable to understand anything, I thought I had injured myself. Afraid, I fell to my knees, begging God's forgiveness if I had done wrong."

"Amiable innocent!" I said at the end of her affecting confession. "You told no one of this experience that was so terrifying to you?"

"I'd not have dared. Until an hour ago, I remained in ignorance of what happened to me that day. But you have revealed the secret to me. Now all is clear."

At this, she rolled onto her back and threw her arms wide, replicating those free and innocent movements that accompanied her first experience of divine release. Desire swept me.

"Oh, Fanny!," I cried. "What that avowal does to me! It makes my cup of felicity to overflow—receive once again this proof of my love."

Turning to Gamiani, I said, "My dear, excite me, please, that I may flood this newborn flower with celestial dew."

No less eager than myself, the wanton Countess laid her head on my thigh and took into her mouth that organ of pleasure with which I intended to convey the same delight to Fanny.

What zeal! What ardor! Time and again, she swallowed my manhood to its very root—then, when I was as ready as any stallion to cover my ravishing dam, it was she who led me to the beautiful child and, after baptizing the organ once more with the juices of her succulent mouth, guided it home to the very fountainhead of pleasure.

"Oh, but how she enjoys it," exclaimed Gamiani.

Covering her face with kisses, she moved her mouth lower to suckle Fanny's breasts, nipping with sharp white teeth at the swollen nipples until the girl whimpered in the sweetness of her pain.

"Alcide!" moaned Fanny. "I am expiring! Alcide . . ."

And sweet voluptuousness drowned us in drunken ecstasy, raising us both to the skies.

• • •

After a brief period of repose our senses grew calm.

"Now, Alcide," said Gamiani. "Since the pattern of our pleasures seems to require an element of the intellect, and not simply the satisfaction of desire, I believe it is time you told us something of your *education sentimentale.*"

"With pleasure," I replied.

alcide's story

"*i was born of young* and robust parents. My childhood was a happy one, free of tears or illness. From the age of thirteen, I may say that I was made like a man, with all that might be necessary in the way of physical attributes to prove it.

"You may understand that those needlings to which the flesh is susceptible made themselves keenly felt in me. And yet, in an irony that you may find amusing, I had been marked out from childhood for as career in the clergy!"

At this, Gamiani raised her famous eyebrow, and even Fanny, drowsing in postcoital languor, snorted softly.

"Believe this or not, as you please, but, having been raised to respect chastity above all things, I concentrated my strength on resisting my senses' earliest desires. I condemned myself to the most austere fasting. If, at night, while I slept, Nature purchased relief on my behalf, this merely stirred up a terror in me. It seemed a disorder, and I guilty of doing nothing to cure it.

"I redoubled my abstinence, and with ever greater attention than before strove to expel every fatal idea. This inner struggle ended by making me dazed, drugged, weary. My enforced continence quickened a sensibility in all my body, or rather produced an irritation I had never experienced before.

"I was often taken by spells of dizziness. It seemed as if objects were spinning, and I with them. Were by chance a young woman to enter my view, she would appear brightly alive, lit, radiant with a fire comparable to electric sparks.

"A strange humor, heated more and more, became too abundant, and rose to my head. The fiery particles that charged it, striking sharply against the windows of my eyes, produced therein a kind of dazzling mirage.

"This state had lasted several months, when, one morning, I suddenly sensed a violent contraction and tension in all my limbs. A dreadful, convulsive movement followed, similar to an epileptic seizure.

"My luminous dazzlings returned with greater force than ever. At first I saw a black circle turn rapidly before me, grow larger, become immense. A piercing light shot from the center of the revolving circle and illuminated it all.

"I discovered an endless horizon; vast inflamed skies traversed by a thousand flying rockets; meteors which then flashed down in golden sprays—sapphire sparks, emerald, azure.

"The fire died out; a bluish, velvety daylight took its place. I swam in a limpid, sweet light, soft as the pale moonbeam of a lovely summer night.

"It was then that, from some very faraway place, there came running toward me, as airy as a swarm of golden butterflies, myriads, infinite hosts of naked girls, fresh and cool and incandescent, translucent too, like alabaster statues.

"I dashed among those subtle creatures, but, laughing and merry, they eluded me, their delicious, frolicking numbers melting for a moment into the blue, then, the next moment, reappearing, still more lively, more joyous; charming bouquets of ravishing faces, every one of which cast a sly smile, a malicious glance my way.

"Some of those sylphs were lively, animated, with fiery looks and trembling breasts. Others were pale and thoughtful, like those virgins of antique times about whom the great poet Ossian wrote. Their frail bodies, voluptuous, were swathed in gauze. These creatures seemed to be dying, to be languishing and expiring, and, though they beckoned to me open-armed, always fled as I approached.

"I played lewdly with myself as I lay upon my couch. My body arched as my frantically trembling hands stroked my glorious priapus. I babbled to myself of love, of pleasures, but in the most indecent terms. My classical education mingling for a moment with my dreams, I beheld Jupiter afire, uprisen, Juno flourishing his glittering thunderbolt. I saw all Olympus in rut, disordered, in a weird melee.

"Then I was witness to an orgy, a hellish bacchanal. In a

dark, deep-lying cavern lit by the red light of evil-smelling torches, blue and green tints reflected hideously upon the bodies of a hundred goat-headed devils, beings of grotesquely obscene form. Some of them, seated in a superbly decorated children's swing, curved through the air, leapt, landed upon a woman, instantly driving their shafts to full depth and producing in her the horrible convulsion of a swift unexpected coupling.

"Others, more mischievous, turned a prudish woman upside down, and each, with an insane laugh, buried a ram's swollen weapon in her, hammering out a din of voluptuous excess. And still others, a lighted taper in their hands, set off a cannon from the barrel of which no explosive shell erupted but instead a gigantic male member which a crazed female devil, steadfast, her thighs wide-flung, received into her body.

"The most wicked of the crew bound a Messalina hand and foot, and, before the lustful eyes of this insatiable nymphomaniac, surrendered themselves to the most flagrant joys and pleasures. Able only to observe, the wretch lay writhing, furious, lips flecked with foam, wild to have that pleasure being denied her.

"Here and there, a thousand miniature demons and imps, each more ugly, more rampant than the other, all skipping and hopping about, went this way, went that, sucking, pinching, nipping, dancing a roundelay, all in a heap. Laughter, spasmodic outbursts everywhere, frenzies, screams, howls, sighs, bodies gone insane, insensible from too much pleasure . . .

"Upon a somewhat higher space, those devils who belonged to the first rank were amusing themselves by parodying the mysteries of our most holy religion.

"A nun, her eye blissfully fixed upon the vaulted ceiling, with devout ardor received the Holy Sacrament—except that the woman was naked and prostrate, the priest a great devil, dressed in ecclesiastical regalia obscenely misarranged, and the white communion host, fixed to the end of the rodlike metal *aspergillum* used to sprinkle holy water, was thrust not into her mouth but into her virgin *sexe*.

"Elsewhere, a little she-devil presented her forehead as if to receive the holy sacrament of baptism, and was rewarded instead by a flood of life's own creamy baptismal liquid, while another, pretending to be dead, was launched into the world beyond not with the solemn last rites of extreme unction and its anointing with holy oils, but with frightful outpourings of the most obscene nature.

"A master-devil, borne upon four shoulders, proudly dandled the most energetic demonstration of his erotico-satanical pleasure, and, during those moments when the spirit moved him, squirted streams of consecrated fluid. Everyone humbled himself as he passed. 'Twas the procession of the Holy Sacrament.

"But then lo! A bell tolled, signaling the end of their rites. The devils called to each other, grasped hands and formed an immense circle. The word was given, the dance began. They turned, went faster, flew lightning-swift. The weakest succumbed or tripped during this violent whirling, this queer galloping absurdity. Their fall sent the others sprawling head-over-heels. It was now no more than a horrible confusion, a grotesque pinwheel of hideous couplings, an unspeakable chaos of battered bodies, all spotted with lust; then there arose a thick mist or smoke which hid it all."

In recalling those dreadful fantasies, I'd closed my eyes, the better to recall them in their fearful vividness. Now, opening them again, I saw Gamiani regarding me quizzically, with Fanny curled as contentedly as a child in the circle of her arm.

"You embroider wonderfully well, Alcide," said the Countess. "Your dream would make a very handsome appearance in a book."

"If this is a book," I said, "there is a postscript. Listen then: what follows is pure reality. . . .

"Freed of these dreadful visions, I felt less burdened but more weary. As I returned to my senses, I found three women, still youthful and clad simply in white dressing gowns, seated beside my bed. I thought my vertigo was still in progress; but I was soon informed that my doctor, having diagnosed my illness, had judged it appropriate to apply the one remedy my case cried out for.

"First of all, I seized a plump white hand and covered it with kisses. Cool rosy lips were pressed upon my mouth. That delicious touch electrified me. I had all the ardor of a man deranged.

"'Oh my lovely ones!' I exclaimed. 'I want to be happy to the ultimate. I want to die in your arms. Lend yourselves to my transports, join me in my madness.'

"And instantly I flung away what still covered me and stretched out full length upon my bed. A pillow was placed under my buttocks; I assumed the most advantageous position. Up soared my device, superb, radiant.

"'You, yes, my dark-haired creature,' I cried, 'you of the breasts so firm and so white, sit at the foot of my bed, extend your legs, let them be close to mine. Excellent! Lift my feet, put them on your breasts, softly rub them upon your pretty love-buttons. Oh, wonderful! Ah, but you are delicious.'

"'Fair-haired one, you with blue eyes, come hither! You shall be my queen. . . . Now, mount up there and sit astride the throne. In one hand take the fire-reddened scepter, hide it, immerse it, set your empire upon it. . . .

"'Hey! Not too quickly! Wait a bit. . . . Go softly to it, rhythmically, like a rider at a slow trot. Prolong the pleasure . . . and you, you so tall, so beautiful, you of the ravishing figure, come put your leg here, sit above my head. . . . 'Tis perfect, you follow me exactly. Spread your thighs, oh farther yet, farther, so that my eye may see you well, my mouth devour you, my tongue penetrate freely into you. But what's this? Stiff and erect! Lower yourself so, give me your breast to kiss.'

"And now, showing her agile tongue, pointed like a Venetian stiletto, the dark-haired one said to her fairer companion: 'Come to me, come to me, let me consume you, your eyes, your mouth. Oh, lewd creature . . . put your hand there, ah now! Softly . . . softly—'

"And so it was each one was moved, was agitated, was excited to pleasure.

"My eyes drank in this busy scene, these lascivious movements, these thoughtlessly assumed, wondrously abandoned attitudes. Cries, moans, sobs mingled, were soon indistinguishable from one another. Fire swam through my veins. My entire being quivered. My hands clutched a burning breast or, frantic, trembling, roved over yet more secret charms. Avidly, I sucked, gnawed, bit. They pleaded with me to stop, that I was killing them, and I only multiplied my efforts.

"That excess finished me. My head fell back heavily. I was without an ounce of strength.

"'Enough! Enough!' I cried. 'Oh, my feet! What incredible ticklings . . . you are hurting me . . . withering me,' and my feet twisted in a cramp.

"For the third time I sensed delirium's approach. I drove with fury, thrust, leapt forward. My three lovely creatures simultaneously lost their balance and control of their senses. I received them, fainting, expiring, in my arms and felt myself being drenched. O joys of Heaven or of Hell! Those unending streams of fire . . ."

This time, it took longer to take leave of those memories, but when I did, it was, as before, to find myself devoured by Gamiani's eyes, though now they burned with a light that was almost evil.

"Ah, Alcide," she said, "what pleasures you have tasted! I envy you."

Looking down at the girl drowsing in her arms, she demanded, "And what of you, Fanny? Why, I do believe the unfeeling creature has fallen asleep."

Fanny stirred drowsily. "Leave me to myself, Gamiani. Take your hand away. It weighs upon me. I am undone, tired to death. . . . What a night it has been! My God. Let's sleep."

"No, no," said the Countess, shaking her, but to no avail. Exasperated, she rose and paced the room, oblivious of her nudity.

"I'm in a very different mood," she said. "I am tormented."

She turned to me urgently. "Don't you see? I want to do it until I drop from absolute exhaustion. Your two bodies, your discourses, our furies—everything stimulates me, carries me away. Hell prowls in my spirit, fire seethes in my body."

Throwing herself back down on the bed, she arranged herself in the most lascivious positions ever imagined by the most inventive pornographer, and begged me to satisfy myself in whatever way I desired.

But it was in vain that I bestowed kisses upon the most sensitive parts of the Countess's body. My hands grew weary from torturing her. My spermatic canals were blocked or emptied. I brought forth blood only; no delirium ensued.

My failure roused Gamiani to fury. "I can stand no more of this, I am burning. You have no idea what agony it is, to fail to enjoy."

Her teeth chattered violently, her eyes rolled in their sockets, all of her trembled. Her entire person was agitated, was bent, warped. It was horrible to see.

"I am leaving you," she said abruptly. "Go to sleep."

"But where? It is deepest night."

"Where I go now or what I do are none of your concern."

With these words, Gamiani sprang from the bed, threw on her peignoir, opened the door, disappeared.

When she didn't return within ten minutes, I shook Fanny awake and explained what had happened.

"I fear she has done herself some injury," I said. "Her manner as she departed was—"

But before I could finish, Fanny stilled me with her hand.

"Hush, Alcide. Listen."

In the silence of the sleeping house, echoing along its corridors, came the sounds of the most agonized screams.

"She is killing herself," I cried. "Great God!"

Covering ourselves with what scraps of clothing we could snatch up, we hurried toward the source of Gamiani's cries. They led us to what I recognized as the room occupied by the Countess's maid, Julie.

Its door was locked, and nobody responded to our pounding, although Gamiani's cries continued unabated. Finally, we pulled a couch to the door, and, standing on it, were able to look into the room through a narrow glass window.

What a spectacle! By the dim light of a flickering night-lamp, we could make out the Countess rolling, howling, upon a large cat-fur rug. A foamy saliva was upon her lips; blood and sperm from the night's excesses wet her thighs.

The feel of animal fur on her body roused her to writhings and feats of agility more familiar in beasts of the jungle than a fashionable Parisian *hotel particulier*. Periodically, she would arch herself up from the floor, supported only on heels and head, then subside, collapsing with a dreadful laugh.

Initially, our limited view suggested the Countess was alone, but a moment later Julie, her maid, emerged from her closet, hands full of silken cords and leather belts. She too, was naked, her stocky physique, pale skin and hair tightly plaited into a single braid hanging down her back, suggesting a woman warrior from the medieval Teutonic myths, a Brunhilde of the boudoir.

Gamiani welcomed her appearance with delight.

"Come to me!" she cooed. "My head is spinning."

Indifferent to her pleas, Julie expertly turned the Countess on her back. Looping a cord around one wrist, she knotted it, then bound that wrist to the corresponding ankle. She repeated the action with the other wrist and ankle, so that the Countless could only lie on her back, knees lifted, thighs wide spread, utterly helpless.

At this indignity, her fury reached its extreme pitch. Her spasms terrified me. Here indeed was a female Prometheus being torn all at once by a hundred vultures.

"Oh, damned creature, crazy one," she snarled at her servant. "I am going to bite you."

Undoubtedly she would have done so, had Julie been

less agile. But it seemed the young maid knew all of her mistress's moods. The scenes we observed had been enacted before in this room, and more than once.

Confirmation came when the Countess turned her attention from Julie and focused it on something just below our vantage point, but out of her sight.

"Médor!" she shouted. "Médor! Take me!"

The appearance at this point of another servant—some well-endowed and priapic groom or gardener—would not have surprised me, but I was shocked, and felt a corresponding start in Fanny which almost dislodged us from our precarious perch, when, in response to her cry, an enormous black dog came into view.

The beast was more than large enough to tear out the throat of the helpless Gamiani, but such was not his intention. Instead, snuffling and panting, he dropped to his belly and, sidling in between her open thighs, ardently fell to licking her clitoris, the point of which protruded, red and inflamed.

What paroxysms of pleasure and pain the rough surface of that animal's tongue and the vigor of his attack roused in this voracious wanton. Soon she was screaming with each new stroke, the nerves of her tenderest flesh abraded by an organ more fitted to tearing apart a living beast and the consumption of its flesh.

"Hai! Hai! Hai!"

Over and over again she screamed, each time matching her tone to the sensation rending her. How could her servants not hear? But perhaps, like Julie, they had been educated to ignore any sound emerging from the Countess's apartments in the depth of night.

In time, sensing from her mistress's state of near collapse that she had, for the moment, endured as much as she could of pleasure, Julie hauled back the dog.

"Milk!" croaked Gamiani. "Bring me milk!"

Could the Countess really desire at such a moment a pleasure so prosaic as a draught of fresh milk? Any such thoughts were soon dispelled, however, when Julie reappeared, bearing an enormous artificial penis which, by means of straps, she buckled around her naked loins.

The most generously endowed stallion in his moment of supremest power could not, at least as regards thickness and volume, have equaled that device. The instrument securely in place, Julie pressed a spring on its side, whereupon it expelled halfway across the room a squirt of what I assumed was warmed milk.

I simply could not believe that even Gamiani's capacious cavity could accommodate so substantial an object. However, to my unlimited astonishment, five or six savage thrusts by Julie sufficed for her mistress, amid wracking, shrill screams, to engulf it so that the pale hair of Julie's pubic bush was interwoven with her mistress's dark luxuriant growth.

In doing so, however, the Countess underwent the sufferings of the damned. Agony turned her body rigid, pale, motionless, as if flesh had become marble, and she the embodiment of Cassini's statue of the prophetess Cassandra.

Julie, braced on hands and knees above the supine body

of her mistress, performed with consummate skill the actions of a lover—a movement which the faithful Médor, dispossessed but as faithful to instruction as ever, interpreted as invitation. The dutiful hound flung himself incontinently upon Julie, whose thighs, opened and in action, yielded a glimpse of the most delicious feast. So well did he wield his skilled tongue that she paused in her ministrations to her mistress and seemed to faint away, overwhelmed by that pleasure which, as a woman's expression betrays in those moments of ecstasy, outdoes all that can be imagined.

Irritated by a delay which prolonged her pain and postponed her satisfaction, the unhappy Countess swore and fumed like a devil from the pit.

Julie, restored to her senses, straightaway began again, and with renewed vigor. The Countess shuddered, strained. She closed her eyes, her mouth gaped, and Julie, recognizing that the instant was approaching, squeezed the trigger which expelled the milky fluid within the writhing Gamiani.

"Ah! Ah, stop. I'm coming!" she cried.

Infernal lust! I stood rooted to the spot.

My reason had deserted me, my gaze was fascinated. Those crazed transports, those brutal delights set my brain to reeling. There was naught left in me but lust for burning, disordered blood, luxury and debauch. I was bestialized, furious with love.

Fanny's face had also undergone a singular alteration. Her regard was fixed, her arms stiff and nervously pressed against me. Her half-separated lips and clenched teeth indicated her expectancy of a delirium of sensuality which borders on the raging paroxysm that calls out for excess.

Indifferent to the pleasure and pain of our hostess, we hurried back to the boudoir. No sooner had we reached the bed than with a leap we sprang at each other, like two maddened animals. Our bodies were everywhere in touch, rubbing together, galvanizing each other rapidly. In the midst of convulsive embraces, hoarsely driven cries, frantic bitings, a hideous coupling took place—a coupling of flesh and nerve and bone, a brutal raw shock, swift, devouring, whence came blood only.

Sleep arrived at last to put a term to those furies.

After five hours of health-giving calm, I was the first to wake. The sun was already up; its rays joyously pierced the curtains and played golden reflections upon the rich tapestries and silken materials with which the room was decorated.

Multicolored and poetic, that enchanted awakening after an unearthly night restored me to my old self. I felt as if I had escaped a frightful nightmare, and I had by me, in my arms, beneath my hand, a sweetly stirring breast, a breast of lily and roses, so youthful, so delicate and so pure that merely to brush it with one's lips was enough to make one fear one had bruised it.

Oh, the delicious creature! Fanny, made newly innocent by sleep, half nude, upon an oriental couch, realized the whole ideal of the most beautiful dream. Her head was resting, gracefully turned, upon her well-rounded arm. Her profile was drawn with smoothness and regularity and purity, like one of Raphael's sketches. Her body, in each of its parts as in its entirety, was of a stunning beauty.

In a leisurely manner to savor the sight of so many charms was itself a very considerable delight, but it was, too, a pity to think that, for this virgin for fifteen springtimes, one single night had sufficed to betray the pure tint of her maidenhood. Freshness, grace, youth: our savage orgy had soiled them all, dirtied each, plunged everything into filth and disfigurement. This soul, so naïve and so tender, was henceforth delivered utterly unto the demon of impurity; no more illusions, no more dreams, no more first love, no more sweet surprises; all the poetic life of the young girl gone, burst, forever lost!

She woke, the poor child, almost laughing. She supposed she was opening her eyes upon her customary morning, her gentle thoughts, her innocence. But alas, she saw me. This was not her bed. This was not her room. The pain I saw in her face! And how it hurt me! Tears choked her. I contemplated her—I, moved, ashamed of myself. I held her tightly squeezed in my arms. And each one of her tears . . . I drank them, enraptured!

My senses were mute, my soul alone spoke, unburdening itself entirely. My love was brightly, hotly painted in my language and in my eyes. Fanny listened to me without saying a word. She was amazed, enchanted. She inhaled my breath, drank in my stare, sometimes hugged me, and seemed to be saying: "Oh, yes! Still yours, I am still all yours." As she had surrendered her body, credulous and innocent, now she also gave up her soul, full of confidence, intoxicated. As we kissed, I imagined I felt her soul upon my lips, and gave her mine, all of it. 'Twas heaven. 'Twas everything.

Finally, we rose.

I wanted to see the Countess again. I found her in her salon, asleep, sprawled on the fragile chaise longue. She was all in an ignoble heap, her face distorted, her body unclean, polluted. Like a drunken woman, naked, flung into a gutter, she seemed to be fermenting in her lewdness.

"Ah, let us leave this place!" I cried. "Let us be gone, Fanny. An end to this vile interlude."

the second night

hoping that fanny, so young, at heart innocent, would preserve nothing but a horrible and disgusted remembrance of Gamiani, I overwhelmed the girl with tenderness and affection, lavishing on her the gentlest, the most tender, the most bewitching caresses. Sometimes I would come close to crushing her with pleasure, for I hoped mightily she would thereafter conceive no passion save that willed by Nature who conjoins the two sexes in the senses' pleasures and the soul's.

Alas! I was mistaken. Her imagination had been struck. What she had beheld that night exceeded all our innocent pleasures. In Fanny's eyes, there was nothing to match her friend's transports. Our warmest couplings seemed chill to her when compared with the furious tumults she had known in the course of that fatal night.

She had sworn to me she would see Gamiani no more, but her oath did not extinguish the desire she secretly harbored. She fought in vain. That inner conflict served only to arouse her all the more. I soon realized she'd not be able to resist.

No longer did she behave naturally and freely in my presence. I had lost her confidence. I had to conceal myself in order to observe her.

By means of a hole in a partition, I was able to keep an eye upon her when each evening she retired to bed. The poor creature! I often saw her weep, despairingly turn and twist upon her couch, and then all of a sudden rip off her clothing, fling it far from her, place her naked self before a mirror, look at herself with the wild eyes of one crazed. She touched, slapped, scratched, excited herself, her mind distracted, her actions frenzied and brutally rough.

I could do no more to cure her, but I wanted to see to what lengths she was driven by her sensual delirium. Revelation was not long to be delayed,

One evening, as I stood at my post, observing Fanny as she undressed for bed, I heard her exclaim, "Who is that? Is it you, Angélique?"

Yet the person who entered was not her maid, but a cloaked and incognito Gamiani!

Though instinct urged me to run immediately to her aid, to burst into her room and eject the interloper, I told myself that, only by observing how Fanny reacted to this renewed temptation, would I truly discover the degree of Gamiani's influence. I resolved therefore to watch and wait.

"Oh, Madame," said Fanny, flustered. Although the two women had been naked together in the most lascivious of situations, Fanny reached for a peignoir to cover her *deshabille*. "I did not know . . ."

"Doubtless," smiled the Countess bitterly. "As you have repeatedly had me sent away, I was forced to resort to a trick. I deceived your servants, lured them away. And here I am."

To her credit, Fanny rallied her resistance, and replied to the Countess most strenuously.

"My refusal to receive you should have advised you in the clearest terms that I do not wish your presence, that I find it odious. I reject you, abhor you. Leave me, I pray; go, avoid a scandal."

But Gamiani was unmoved. "My decision is made. You'll not change it, Fanny. My patience has worn thin!"

"Indeed! What do you intend to do? Constrain me again, use violence upon me, soil me? Madame, you will either leave or I will summon aid."

Ignoring these protestations, Gamiani, still wrapped in her cloak, subsided gracefully into a chair.

"We are alone, my child; the doors are locked, I've thrown the keys through the window into the garden. You are mine. But be calm. You have nothing to fear."

She reached out for my darling, but Fanny recoiled. "For God's sake don't touch me!"

"Fanny, it will do no good to resist. You will succumb one way or another. Of us two, I am the stronger, and passion stirs me. A man would not be able to defeat me."

The emotions conflicting in Fanny's breast overcame her, and she sank weakly to her bed. In an instant, Gamiani was seated beside her.

"Why! She trembles," she murmured. "grows pale. Dear God! Fanny, my Fanny. What have I done? Open your eyes, wake up! Wake."

Like one under the influence of a noxious drug, Fanny half opened her eyes.

"If I press you thus," murmured Gamiani, "it is for love of you. You are my life, my soul. I'm not wicked, evil; no, my little one, my darling. No, I am good, very good, for I love you. Look into my eyes."

Taking Fanny's limp hand, she laid it on her breast.

"Feel how my heart beats. It beats for you, for no one else! I wish for your joy only, your drunkenness in my embrace. Come back to me, come back to life; let me kiss you from sleep."

"You will be the death of me," moaned Fanny. "My God! Leave me—you are horrible!"

"Horrible?" said Gamiani. "What in me can inspire horror? Am I not still young? Am I not beautiful too? I am everywhere said to be. And my heart! Is it capable of a greater love? That fire which consumes me, which eats me alive, that blazing Italian fire which redoubles my sensitivity and makes victorious where all others give way, fail, yield, is that fire then something horrible?"

Warming to her subject, the Countess knelt by the bed and lectured Fanny her as a loving aunt might a wayward niece.

"Tell me, what is a man, a lover, in comparison with me? Two or three bouts and he is done, overthrown. The fourth, and he gasps his impotence and his loins buckle.

Pitiful thing! I remain strong, trembling, I remain unappeased. I personify the ardent joys of matter, the burning joys of the flesh. Luxurious, lewd, implacable, I give unending pleasure, I am love itself, love that slays!"

"Enough, Gamiani," said Fanny. "I have had enough of this."

"No, no. Listen to me yet, Fanny, hear me out. To be naked, to sense oneself young and beautiful, smooth, sensual, to burn with love and shudder with pleasure; to touch, to mingle, to exhale body and soul in a sigh, a single cry, a cry of love . . . Fanny! Fanny, that is Heaven."

"Oh, have mercy upon me!" cried Fanny. "I am weak. You weave a spell over me. You insinuate yourself into my flesh, you pierce my bones, you are a poison. Oh, yes! You are horror and . . ."

She turned to face her tormentor, and her resolve cracked. "And I love you."

The color drained from Gamiani's face; she was motionless. Her eyes wide open, her hands clasped, upon her knees before Fanny, it seemed as if she had been suddenly turned to stone. She was sublime in annihilation and ecstasy.

"Say those words again!" she demanded. "Repeat it, that burning word."

"Yes! Yes!" cried Fanny. "I love you with all my body's strength. I want you, I desire you. Oh, I shall lose my mind over you!"

In an instant, Gamiani was on her feet and embracing the girl.

"Your hair is beautiful," she crooned. "How soft it is. It slips through my fingers, fine, silken, aglow. Your brow is pure, whiter than the lily. You are fair of skin, satin-smooth, perfumed, celestial from head to foot. You are an angel, you are voluptuousness itself."

Expertly, she slipped her hands inside Fanny's bodice, cupping her breasts, teasing the nipples which I knew would be springing eagerly erect.

"Oh, let those roses show themselves," she begged. "Undo those stay-laces, be naked. . . ."

She shrugged off her cloak, to reveal herself naked beneath it.

"Quick. I am nude already."

In an instant, Fanny too was in the state of nature.

"Stand there. Let me admire you," said the Countess. "If only I were able to paint you; to immortalize a single one of your features . . ."

She caressed Fanny in a frenzy of lust.

"Let me kiss your feet, your knees, your breast, your mouth. Embrace me, oh, squeeze me."

Like one succumbing to the influence of a noxious potion, Fanny put her arms around her tormentor.

"Harder! What joy! What joy! She loves me."

So close was their embrace that their bodies seemed to have become united. Only their heads remained apart. They looked at each other with ravished expressions. Their eyes glanced fire, their cheeks were flushed crimson.

Even then, however, in the depth of her lust, Fanny yet

kept some sense of the innocence she had experienced for a moment with me, but now lost, perhaps forever.

"I have been happy," she said wistfully. "Very happy."

But Gamiani replied with the cunning of Satan himself.

"I too, my own Fanny, and full of happiness unknown to me before this. The soul and the senses met upon your lips. Come to your bed, and let us taste a night of drunkenness."

Fanny, naked, fell upon the bed, stretched out, lay back voluptuously. Gamiani, kneeling on the rug, drew her to her breast, wrapped her arms around the girl.

Speechless, she contemplated her victim. Kisses replied to kisses. Hands flew; adept, agile hands. Flushed, animated by pleasure's searing fire, both appeared, to my eyes, to be sparkling. Thanks to rage and passion, those two delirious furies were, so to speak, making a poem of the excess of their debauch; simultaneously, they addressed the senses and the imagination.

In vain I reasoned with myself, condemned those absurd extravagances, since I was soon myself roused and hot, possessed by desires. Prevented as I was from dashing in and joining them, I resembled a wild beast in heat whose eyes devour his female counterpart, separated from him by his cage's bars.

Stupefied, my head glued to the partition, my eye to the aperture whence as it were I inhaled my torture, I experienced the true agony of the damned: terrible, unbearable torture which first assails the head, the mind, then infuses itself into the blood, next infiltrates the bones to their marrow which it does not cease to scorch.

I could no longer breathe; foam appeared on my lips. I lost my head. I became mad, furious, and in a rage grasping my virility, I felt the whole of my man's strength thrash furiously between my tensed fingers, throb for an instant, then burst, and issue in blazing jets like a fiery spray.

Having collected myself, I found I was exhausted. My eyelids were heavy. I could barely hold my head erect. I wanted to retreat from my vantage point, but a sigh expelled by Fanny held me riveted there. I was in thrall to the demon of the carnal. While my hands worked to revive my faded power, I punished my eyes by contemplating the very scene which so horrified me.

Now the legs of my nymphomaniacs were dovetailed in such a way that their tufted down met squarely; each was rubbing her vagina upon the other's. They attacked, mutually thrust at one another, drove with an obstinacy and a vigor only the nearing approach of pleasure can produce in women. One would have thought they wished to be split in half or exploded, so violent were their efforts, so hoarse was their panting respiration.

Fanny whimpered, "I can stand no more, I am being maimed and slaughtered!"

"Then come." Joining two fingers, Gamiani slid them within Fanny's vagina. "Push! Here it is! Here it is. . . ."

Fanny wriggled at this new and delicious penetration. "I think I am being set afire. Oh, I feel it flow! "

As Fanny spent in glorious passion, Gamiani bit the sheets, clawed, chewed the hair floating about her face. Lost in my own lust, I followed their outbursts, their moans reached my ears; until, like them, I attained the summit of delight.

"Oh, I am dead from weariness!" whispered Gamiani. The color had drained from her face. She was motionless, her eyes wide open, her hands joined, upon her knees before Fanny. It seemed as if she had been suddenly heavenstruck and turned to stone. She was sublime in annihilation and ecstasy.

"I am broken," replied Fanny, "but what pleasures I have tasted!"

"The longer the effort, and the more painful, the more keen and prolonged the enjoyment, the spasm."

"I have experienced it. For more than five minutes, I was drowned in a kind of intoxicating dizziness. The irritation extended into every one of my fibers. That rubbing of hair against skin so tender it caused me frightfully to itch, I rolled myself in fire, in sensual joy. O madness! O happiness! To take one's pleasure! To ejaculate! Oh, I understand the word now: pleasure!"

Her thirst for satisfaction sated now, Fanny resumed the manner of her former innocence, and with it a child's inquisitiveness.

"Gamiani, one thing does astonish me. How is it that, young as you are, you are yet so experienced? I should never have dreamt of all the wild things we have done. Whence does your knowledge come? What are the origins of this passion of yours which is my undoing, which sometimes terrifies me? I don't believe you were born this way. Nature does not create us in this sort."

Gamiani, also briefly free of desire, assumed a role in which I had not before seen here—that of teacher.

"I see that you wish to know who I am," she said. "Ah well! Hug me in your arms, let's link our legs, press against each other. I'll tell you about my life at the convent. It's a story which will probably inflame us, give us further desires."

Fanny snuggled up to her. "I am listening."

"You've not forgotten," began Gamiani, "the atrocious ordeal my aunt made me undergo in the interests of her lechery. I had no sooner realized the horror of her conduct than I pilfered some of her documents which would be the guarantee of my fortune. I also took some jewels and some money and, profiting from a moment when that worthy lady was absent, I left to seek refuge in the convent of the Sisters of Redemption.

"No doubt touched by my youth and my apparent shyness, the Mother Superior gave me the warmest possible welcome, which was calculated to dissipate my fears and help me overcome my embarrassment.

"I related what had happened to me. I asked for asylum, and requested her protection. She took me in her arms, hugged me affectionately and called me her daughter. After that she described the sweet tranquillity of life in the convent. She added fuel to my hatred for men, and ended with an exhortation so pious in its language that it seemed to me it could only have emanated from a divine spirit.

"In order that the abrupt transition from worldly life to that of the cloister be rendered less extreme, it was decided

I would remain close to the Mother Superior and would sleep each night in her cell. Things went splendidly; by the second night we were chatting together in the most familiar way.

"In bed, the Mother began to toss and turn. This continued a long time. She complained of being cold, and besought me to lie with her and avail her of my warmth. I found her absolutely naked. 'One sleeps more soundly,' she explained, 'when unencumbered by a nightgown.' She suggested I remove mine; I did so to please her.

"'Oh, my little one,' cried she, fingering me, 'your skin is burning—and how soft it is! The barbarians who dared molest you in that way! You must have suffered atrociously. Tell me just what they did to you. They beat you, you say?'

"I repeated my story in all its details, emphasizing those which seemed to interest her the most. She took such a keen pleasure in hearing me speak that she was soon quivering in an extraordinary manner. 'Poor child! Poor child!' she reiterated, clutching me with all her strength.

"I knew not how it came to pass but I gradually found myself lying on top of her. Her legs were wrapped around my waist, her arms surrounded me. A tepid, penetrating warmth spread through my frame. I felt an unknown ease, a delicious comfort which communicated to my bones, to my flesh, I cannot tell you what love-sweat which flowed in me with a milky sweetness.

"'You are kind, you are very good to me,' I told her. 'I love you. I am happy here beside you. I never want to be away from you. 'My mouth glued itself to her lips, and with much passion I continued: 'Oh, yes! I love you so much I feel as if I were dying of love. . . . I don't know . . . but I feel . . .'"

The Mother Superior stroked me slowly. Her body squirmed, wriggled, but sweetly, beneath mine. Her stiff woolly fleece brushed mine, stung, pricked me sharply, roused up a perfectly divine tickling sensation. I was out of my mind from this devilry. I shivered so much my whole body quaked.

"At this, she flung me a violent kiss. 'Oh, my God!' I cried, 'no more,' and never did dew fall more abundantly, more deliciously after any love-combat that ever there was.

"The ecstasy passed. Far from exhausted, I flung myself with redoubled zeal upon my companion. I ate her alive with caresses. I took her hand and conveyed it to the place she had just so powerfully irritated. The Mother, seeing me thus, forgot herself altogether and began to behave like a bacchante. Our ardors, our kisses, our bites competed vigorously.

"Oh, what agility, what suppleness were in that woman's limbs. Her body curved, arched, straightened with a snap, rolled; it drove me mad. I was no longer in control of myself. I had scarce enough time to return a kiss, so thickly did hers rain down upon me, covering from head to foot. It seemed as if I were being eaten, devoured in a thousand separate places! That incredible activity, that tempest of lubricious fondlings put me in a state I cannot possibly describe. Oh Fanny, if only you could have been there to witness our assaults, our outbursts! Had you but seen us two, furious, panting, you would have been able to understand all that may occur when two women in love are under the sway of their senses.

"In an instant, my head was gripped between my wrestling-companion's thighs. I divined her desires. Inspired by lust, I fell to gnawing upon her most sensitive parts. But I ill complied with her wishes. Quickly, she eluded me, slid out from under my body and, suddenly spreading my own thighs, immediately attacked me with her mouth. Her pointed, nervous tongue stabbed at me. Her teeth closed upon me and seemed about to tear me.

"I began to fling about as if I were doomed. I thrust the Mother's head away, I dragged her by the hair. Then she let go: she touched me softly, injected saliva into me, licked me slowly, or mildly nipped my hairs and flesh with a refinement so delicate and at the same time so sensual that the very thought of it makes me come this minute with pleasure.

"Oh! What delights made me drunk! What a rage held me in its grip! I screamed and shouted unendingly. I fought, fell stricken, was raised up, it began again, and always the swift-moving, sharp-pointed tongue found me, ran stiffly into me. Two thin, firm lips took my clitoris, pinched it, kneaded it in such a way I thought I should die.

"No, Fanny, it is not possible to feel that, to enjoy oneself that way more than once in a lifetime. That indescribable nervous tension, the blood pounding in my swollen arteries; what heat in my flesh, what fire in my blood! I was burning, I tell you, I was like metal in the forge, pounded by the hammer of a lust made so insatiable as to extract my very essence. White hot, I desired to be quenched, to be plunged into blood and oil as did the great armorers with their weapons of steel, to render it unbreakable and induce the keenest edge.

"But how happy I was! Fanny! Fanny! I can restrain myself not another second! As I speak to you of those excesses I think I can again feel those same consuming titillations— finish me. . . ."

Fanny parted Gamiani's thighs and thrust her mouth as hungrily onto her tender part as a famished she-wolf on her prey.

"Quicker, harder," begged the Countess. "Good, ah, good! Ah! I am dying." But even when she was spent, Fanny continued greedily to gorge herself.

"Enough! Enough!" Gamiani cried. "You're sucking me dry, you devilish creature! I'd have sworn you were less skillful, less passionate. Ah, but I see what we have here. You're developing. The fire is in you."

"But how could it not be?" demanded Fanny. "One should have to be deprived of blood and life to remain insensible with you. Tell me, then, tell me, what did you do next?"

"Thereafter nothing hindered us," said Gamiani. "All restraint was banished, and I soon learned that the nuns of the convent of Redemption were given to collective worship of sensuality; that they had a secret place where they assembled for their orgies, where they sported at their ease. The service opened at the hour of Compline and was finished by that of Matins.

"What I heard appalled me to such a point I beheld the Mother Superior as Satan incarnate. However, she reassured me, murmured a few compliments in my ear and above all diverted me by relating how she had lost her maidenhead. You'd never guess to whom it was that priceless treasure was given. The tale is a strange one and is well worth the trouble to tell.

"The Mother Superior, whom from now on I shall call Sainte, was the daughter of a ship's captain. Her mother, an intelligent and educated woman, had brought her up in all the principles of our sacred belief, which, however, by no means prevented young Sainte's erotic temperament from developing at an early age.

"When she was twelve she was rocked by intolerably fierce desires. These she sought to satisfy by every bizarre means a roving imagination could devise.

"The unhappy girl labored over herself every night. Her untaught and inadequate fingers spoiled her youth and ruined her health. She one day clapped eyes on two dogs in the act of holding amorous commerce. Her lewd curiosity led her to observe the mechanism and action, and henceforth she had a better idea of what she was lacking.

"Living as she was in an isolated house, surrounded by elderly servants, never seeing a man, how could she ever hope to come upon that living arrow, so red and so swift, which had seemed so very wonderful to her and which she supposed must similarly exist for women?

"It finally occurred to her that, of all animals, the ape most closely resembles man. And indeed her voyaging father owned a superb orang-utan. She visited its cage to study it, and as her examination was of considerable length, the beast, aroused by the girl's proximity, manifested a device of the most brilliant category.

"Sainte leapt for joy. She had at last found what she had always been seeking, that about which she had dreamt every night. Her ideal appeared there before her eyes, visible, touchable. Better still, the unspeakable jewel was springing erect in a more solid, more ardent, more threatening fashion than she had ever visualized in her most ambitious moments.

"She devoured it with her eyes. The ape approached, clung to the bars and exhibited himself so dramatically that poor Sainte went quite out of her head. Driven by madness, she forced aside one of the cage's bars and created a space wide enough to allow the lusty beast to make the most of his good humor. Eight honest, well-pronounced inches shot forth.

"At first, this extravagant wealth terrified our maiden. Nevertheless, urged on by the devil, she dared a closer look. Her hand found the miracle, caressed it. The ape trembled, the bars shook. The beast's grimace was perfectly dreadful. Terrified, Sainte believed this was Satan leering at her. Fear restrained her.

"She was about to retreat when a final glance cast upon the flamboyant bait reawakened every one of her desires. She became emboldened at once. With a resolute air, she lifted her skirts and bravely backed up to the animal, her behind aimed at the redoubtable point.

"You may imagine the scene. The battle was joined, blows struck. Inspired, Beast rose gloriously to the level of Man. Sainte was embestialized, devirginated, enmonkeyed! Her joy, her transports exploded in a chorus of ohs and ahs, but the lass sang with such gusto her mother overheard and, recognizing the tune, came running, to surprise her daughter, well buttered, struggling skewered on the blade!"

Fanny clapped her hands in delight, for all the world like a child watching a *guignol* in the Jardins du Luxembourg.

"Superb farce."

"So, to cut a long story short, to cure the poor girl of her monkeymania, she was installed in a convent."

Showing a coarseness I would not have expected in one so young or carefully raised, Fanny giggled. "'Better to have left her free to bump bellies with a jungle full of monkeys."

"You'll soon see how right you are," said Gamiani.

Taking up her story once more, she continued. "My temperament willingly adapted itself to the convent's life of feasts and pleasures. Very joyfully, most willingly I consented to be initiated into the mysteries of monastic saturnalias. My admission having been accepted by the chapter, I was presented two days later.

"According to the rules, I arrived naked. I took the required oath, and to complete the ceremony I courageously prostituted myself to an enormous wooden priapus, a monster with dimensions comparable to the muscular forearm of a blacksmith.

"I had no sooner finished that painful penetration when a band of nuns descended upon me with all the impetuosity of a tribe of cannibals. I lent myself to every caprice. I struck the most lubricious attitudes, finally ending with an obscene dance, after which those present acclaimed me their equal. I was exhausted.

"A very lively little nun, wide awake, alert and more refined than the Mother Superior, conducted me to her bed. She was by far the most thorough-going nymphomaniac ever bred by Hell. I conceived a carnal passion for her, and we were almost always together during the vast nocturnal routs."

"Where were these held?" demanded Fanny.

"In a spacious hall, which art and the genius of depravity had been pleased to decorate in the most lavish manner. One arrived there by way of two doors closed off in the oriental fashion by rich draperies edged with gold fringe, ornamented with a thousand curious designs. The walls were hung in dark blue velvet, framed by lemon-wood wainscotting, most artfully carved. Large mirrors, set at equal distances around the walls, rose from floor to ceiling, so that the nude groups of delirious nuns were reflected, during the orgies, in a thousand forms, or rather seemed to spring out, glittering and alive, from between the tapestried panels.

"Cushions, hassocks, pillows, couches took the place of

chairs, and better served lust's frolickings and lechery's postures. A doubly thick rug, made of delicate material and delightful to the touch, covered the floor. Woven into the carpet, with an amazing magic of color, were twenty amorous groups in lascivious attitudes, all very suitable to whet jaded desires, revive surfeited appetites. Elsewhere— in paintings, upon the ceiling—the eye discovered the most eloquent representations of extravagance and abandoned debauchery."

"That must have been delicious," said Fanny. "To see all those things!"

"To that luxury of decoration, add the intoxication of perfumes and flowers," said Gamiani. "A steady, temperate warmth, a tender, mysterious illumination provided by six lamps of alabaster, sweeter than an opal's reflection—all that induced a vague enchantment, mingled with a troubling desire, like a sensual daydream. It was Asia—its luxuriance, its poetry, its careless, unstudied voluptuousness. It was the mystery of the harem; its secret delights, and, above all else, its ineffable languor."

"How sweet, to spend nights of drunkenness there with one's beloved."

Gamaini smiled thinly. "Doubtless Love would willingly have taken up his abode there," she said, "had it not been for the noisy and filthy orgy which, every night, transformed the place into an ungodly stew, a nest of horrors."

"Tell me more of that!" cried an eager Fanny, now hungry for every lubricious detail.

"The midnight hour would sound, and thereupon the

nuns would enter. Each was clad in a simple black tunic which emphasized the whiteness of her skin. Each had bare feet, loose-floating hair. A splendid supper was soon laid. But not for that unholy repast the frugality and solemn silence of the convent meal; the sacred readings that accompany it, augmenting physical sustenance with food for the spirit. Here, once the Mother Superior gave the signal, one ate as one wished. Some remained seated, others reclined upon pillows. Exquisite meats, warm, stimulating wines were consumed in a flash; everyone had a terrible hunger.

"Those women's faces, worn by excess and abuse, cold, pale as daylight, would take on color, would gradually become flushed. Bacchic incenses, aphrodisiac philtres injected fire into the body, trouble into the mind. Conversation waxed lively, became a confused humming, but always ended in obscene remarks, delirious provocations, teasings wrapped in song; laughter, outbursts; the crash of glasses and the bursting of wine bottles and decanters.

"The most feverish nun, she in the greatest haste, would suddenly fall upon her neighbor and bestow a violent kiss which had the effect of galvanizing the entire assembly. Couples formed at once, became entangled, twisted in frantic embraces. Stifled moans, sighs would begin to resound through the room, anguished groans, cries of ardor or prostration. Soon cheeks, breasts, shoulders would appear no longer to suffice as objects for the unrestrained kisses. Dresses were lifted or tossed aside.

"Then one beheld a unique spectacle: nothing but female bodies, supple, graceful, interlocked, stirring, pressing, straining, moving with skill and adroitness, with consummate impetuousness and refinement and lust.

"If the excess of pleasure were not precisely to the satisfaction of impatient desire, a woman might detach herself for an instant in order to recover her breath. She and her partner would regard one another with smoldering eyes, and they would fight to achieve the most lascivious poses, the most enticing gestures or looks. She of the two who triumphed through seduction and debauch would suddenly see her beloved melt, fall upon her, fling her over, cover her with kisses and suckings, eat her with caresses, devour her even to the center of the most secret pleasures, at all times placing herself in such a way as to be able to receive the same attacks. The two heads would become buried between thighs, there would now be only one agitated, convulsively tormented body, whence a low, throaty gasp of lubricious joy would escape, to be followed by a double scream of happiness.

"'They're coming! They're coming!' those doomed nuns would immediately cry in chorus. And they who were made to do the like would leap wild-eyed upon each other, more furious than beasts let free in an arena.

"Eager to know pleasure, they would undertake the most strenuous enterprise, the groups crashing against each other, to fall willy-nilly to the floor, panting, finished, tired of orgy, exhausted from lust; a macabre confusion of nude women, swooning, gasping, heaped together in the most ignominious disorder upon which often, the first glow of daybreak would shine."

"What madness!" said Fanny.

"They didn't limit themselves to that. Their caprices were infinitely various. Deprived of men, we were on that account only the more ingenious at devising new stunts. All the priapic instruments, every one of antiquity's obscene tales and those of modern times were well known to us. We had gone far beyond them. Elephantis and Aretino had no such imaginations as we.

"It would take too long to enumerate our artifices, our stratagems, our potions, marvelously compounded to revive failing strength, waken the desires and satisfy them. You will be able to judge by the treatment to which we exposed any of our number in an effort to needle her, prick up her desires.

"She was first of all plunged into a bath of heated animal's blood—that to quicken her vigor. Next, an aphrodisiac potion was administered; after which she lay down on a bed and every inch of her body was massaged. Next, she was put to sleep by hypnotism. As soon as she had fallen into slumber, her body was adjusted in an advantageous position and she was whipped till she bled. She was pricked with pointed instruments as well.

"Once, the patient woke in the middle of the process. Entranced, wild-eyed, she lifted herself up, stared at us with an insane expression and straightaway suffered the most violent paroxysms. Six persons had trouble keeping her under control. Only a dog's tonguing was able to pacify her. Her fury burst out in torrents. But were it to happen that relief did not come, the wretched one's state would worsen, and in all probability she would cry out for an ass."

"What! An ass? For shame!!"

"Yes, my dear, an ass. We had two, very nicely furnished, and each very docile. We wished to do no less than those Roman ladies who employed them in their saturnalias.

"The first time I was put to the test, I was delirious from wine. Defying all my sisters, I flung myself upon the table used during this particular ceremony. With the aid of a block and tackle the beast was hoisted into position and prepared before my eyes. His awe-inspiring shaft, warmed by the nuns' handling, thudded heavily against my flank.

"I took his colossus in both hands, placed it at my aperture and during several moments of fondling strove to insert it. With the help of dilating ointment, I was soon mistress of at least five brave inches.

"It seemed as if my skin were being ripped, as if I were being split asunder, quartered. The pain was numbing, stifling. But with it was mixed a fiery irritation, titillating and sensual. I wanted to push some more but lacked the strength, and fell back. But the beast, constantly in motion, produced a friction so vigorous my entire spinal column was rattled. My spermatic ducts opened wide and gushed their contents. The burning juice quivered for an instant within my loins—oh! What joy! And how I came! I sensed it race out in spurts and flaming jets, and fall, drop by drop, to the depths of my vagina. I was streaming with love. I emitted a prolonged cry of exhaustion.

"Exhausted, aching in all my limbs, racked with pain, I thought my pleasures over when the intractable rod stiffened more handsomely than before, probed me and nearly lifted me from the table. My nerves swelled, I gritted and ground my teeth; my arms strained as I lifted my thighs to my breasts and spread them wide.

"All of a sudden, a jet inundated me with a hot and sticky rain, so strong, so abundant it seemed to engorge my veins and touch my very heart. My flesh, relaxed and eased by that generous balm, gloried in a satisfaction that penetrated to the bone, the marrow, the brain and the nerves, dissolved my joints into a single flaming essence. Delicious torture, intolerable voluptuousness that unties what binds life together and causes you to die in drunkenness!

"By means of these lubricious capers, I found I had gained an additional two inches of meat. All measure had been exceeded, all record eclipsed; my companions acknowledged defeat."

Fanny was elated. "What transports you provoke in me, Gamiani! I'll soon be able to contain myself no longer. . . . Well, how was it you finally got out of that devilish convent?"

"It happened thus. After a great orgy, we had the idea to transform ourselves, with the aid of artificial penises, into men: to impale each other in such a manner as to be joined into an unbroken line, and then to have a dance.

"I formed the chain's last link; I was, that is to say, the only one who rode horseback but had no rider. Imagine my surprise when I felt myself assaulted by a naked man who had, I've no idea how, got into our midst. I cried out in fright. The line of nuns broke at once. They savagely attacked the unfortunate intruder—not from hatred, but from a desire to satisfy themselves with a true penis where artifice had failed.

"Poor man! Unequal to the demands of twenty voracious sisters, his pathetic organ was soon drained. You should have seen his state of exhaustion; his member was flabby, it dangled, all virility spent. I could barely coax a drop from him when my turn came. I succeeded nevertheless. Lying prone upon the dying fellow, my head lodged between his thighs, I put such skill and deftness into sucking the sleeping Monsieur Priapus that he woke flushed, rubicund, vivacious and fit to give pleasure. Myself caressed by an agile tongue, I soon sensed the oncoming of an incredible pleasure, and I finished it by taking my seat gloriously and with delight upon the scepter I had just made mine by right of conquest. I gave and received a deluge of delight.

"This last excess overwhelmed our gentleman. Nothing succeeded in bringing him back to life. Would you believe it? As soon as the nuns realized the wretch was no longer useful for their purposes, they decided, without a moment's hesitation, to kill him and bury his remains in the cellar, for fear he might compromise the convent. I argued against the criminal decision, but to no end; instantly, a lamp was lowered and detached from its cord, a hangman's knot was made, and the victim strung up.

"I turned away from the horrible sight. . . . But what was this? To those furies' boundless surprise, the hanging produced its customary effect—a postmortem erection. Astounded by this demonstration of the nervous system in its final spasm of life, the Mother Superior mounted a ladder and, to the frantic applause of her accomplices, coupled in midair with the dead man!

"The story does not end there. Too slender or too frayed to support the weight of two, the rope parted. Dead and living tumbled to the floor, so rudely that the Mother Superior broke a bone, while the hanged man, imperfectly strangled, returned to life, his miraculously enlarged member threatening, in his agitated state, to choke the Mother Superior.

"A bolt of lightning sizzling into the crowd would have produced less of an effect than did this scene upon the good sisters. They all fled in terror, believing the devil had come into their company. The Mother Superior alone remained to wrestle with this personage whose resuscitation had been so little expected."

"But yet you abandoned the convent," said Fanny. "How did this come about?"

"Such excesses as this hanging," said Gamiani, "were certain, I sensed, to have dreadful consequences. To avoid them, I escaped that same night from this den of crimes and debauchery.

"I took refuge for a time in Florence. In this city of love

and splendor, a young Englishman, Sir Edward, a dreamer and lover of beauty, conceived a violent passion for me. Until then, my body alone had been agitated. My soul slept on. It woke sweetly to the pure accents, the enchanting notes of a noble and elevated love. From that moment on, I lived a new existence. I experienced those vague, ineffable desires that give to life its happiness and poetry.

"Gunpowder will not not burn of its own accord, but only let a spark come near and it explodes. Thus did my heart catch fire, ignited by the transports of him who loved me. Edward's voice held an intonation that stirred me. The pure language of emotion, new to me, aroused a delicious trembling. I lent an attentive ear. My eager eyes allowed nothing to go unnoticed. The flame that sprang from my lover's eyes penetrated mine and reached to the depths of my soul, whereunto it brought anxiety, delirium, joy. Affection seemed to me painted in his every gesture. All his features, all his traits, animated by passion, found a sympathetic echo in me.

"Edward had one of those powerful spirits that draw others into their sphere. I was raised up to his height. Thus, the first glimpse I had of love made me love the object that offered it to me. Apt to be extreme in all things, I was as ardent to know the life of the heart as I had been to experience that of the senses. My love was exalted. Already idealized, it became sublime, to the extent that the very thought of coarse pleasure revolted me. Edward passionately wished it, but had I been forced to make love, I should have died of rage.

"Frustrated by this deliberately raised barrier, his desire and mine became, under constraint, all the more inflamed. Edward was the first to succumb. Weary of a philosophical high-mindesness, the cause of which he was unable to fathom, he was helpless to resist what his senses urged. He surprised me one day as I lay sleeping and, while I slept, possessed me.

"I woke in the midst of the warmest embraces, and, overcome, joined my pleasures with those of the man in whom I had inspired them. Three times I was raised to Heaven, and Edward was three times a god. But when he had fallen, I conceived a horror of him: a horror of his mortality. He became for me no god, just a man, a creature of flesh and bone, no different from the monks who had debauched me.

"The prism was shattered. An impure breath had extinguished that gleam of love, that Heaven-sent ray which shines but once in a lifetime. My soul existed no longer. The senses surged to life. They alone were alive, so I lived only for them, resuming my former way of life."

"You returned directly to women?" demanded Fanny.

"Not at all! I wished first of all to break with men. In order to have an end to desires and regret, I sipped all the pleasure they could give me. I drank the cup to its dregs.

"Placing myself in the hands of a celebrated matchmaker, I made myself available to every man in Florence who desired to find a wife. The most vigorous of the city's sportsmen had me one after the other. Six athletes were beaten and broken on the track. I, on other hand, in a single morning, could saddle up for thirty-six races and still be ready to return to the starting gate.

"At one point, in the company of three valiant champions, I so amused them with my conversation and manner that a diabolic idea entered my head. To put it into practice and make the most of it, I ordered the strongest to lie on his back and, while I caroused with his sturdy machine and was nimbly sodomized by the second, I got the third into my mouth and caused him such delight that he cried out with pleasure. At this, all three of them and myself as well climaxed at once, like four horses crossing the finish line at the same moment.

"What jockeys! What warmth and cheer in my palace! Can you picture those raptures? To have a mouth capable of draining away every drop of a man's potency, and the thirst to drink it; to swallow floods of warm, acrid cum and, at the same time, to feel two jets of fire traverse you in either direction and gouge your flesh—the pleasure of such a three-fold orgasm is beyond human power to describe! And what's more, my incomparable gymnasts had the generous sportsmanship to repeat it until they collapsed, their strength extinguished."

Gamiani smiled at the memory, but good humor soon left her face.

"Since then," she concluded, "fatigued, disgusted with men, I have not been able to appreciate any desire, any happiness save that of being entwined, nude, with the frail and trembling body of a timid girl, still a virgin, whom one

instructs, whom one initiates and devastates with voluptuousness. . . ."

Her reverie was interrupted by an agitated movement
from young Fanny.

"But . . . what is the trouble? What are you doing?"

"Oh, Gamiani, the desires you rouse in me!" said the
girl. "Horrible desires, monstrous ones. All the pleasure
and all the pain you have felt . . . I too wish to feel it—
now—at once. I want to die of excess, I tell you; I want to
come—come, yes, enjoy! Enjoy!"

"Calm yourself, Fanny!" said Gamiani sharply. "I shall
obey you. What is it you wish?"

"I want—oh, I want your mouth to fasten upon me, I
want it to suck me."

Gamiani needed no further encouragement. Within seconds, her face was buried between the thighs of my
beloved, her tongue probing her innermost folds.

"There!" cried Fanny in a torment of pleasure. "Draw out
my soul! Suck it out!"

For long moments, I watched Gamiani rouse Fanny
again and again to climax, until even the girl could no
longer endure the protracted pleasure, and pushed away
her still-eager partner.

"Now I want to lay hands on you," said Fanny, "slide my
fingers deep into you and make you scream as you did me."

She shivered in a delirium of desire. "Oh, that ass! He
torments me too. I should like to have an enormous member, I care not how immense or whether it should split me,
burst me!"

"Then you will be satisfied, my wild creature. Here he is—or something very like."

She produced that dreadful instrument we had seen Julie use upon her.

"Ah, what a monster!" said Fanny, stroking the monstrous object. "Give it to me right away. I want to try it."

Snatching it, she attempted to force it into her vagina, but quickly desisted, sobbing with pain and frustration.

"Impossible! It will never go in!"

"You must first know how to guide it," said Gamiani. "Lie down belly up, my dear. Stretch out, spread your sweet thighs; spread them wide. Let your arms fall listlessly down. Surrender yourself with neither fear nor reservation."

"Oh yes, yes! I'll surrender myself joyfully! Put it into me, quickly!"

But Gamiani would not be hurried. I sensed that, having completed the first stage of her initation, Fanny was about to be raised to the next circle of that Hell, closer to the cold heat of the Countess's own nymphomania.

"Patience, my child!" she murmured. "Listen to me. In order to experience every part of the pleasure with which I am about to make you reel, you must forget yourself completely. You must lose yourself, limit your consciousness to one thing only, to thoughts of sensual love, to carnal and delirious enjoyment.

"No matter how I attack you, or how passionately I become aroused, do not move. Remain still, receive my kisses without returning them. If I bite you, if I tear your flesh, suppress the sob of pain, just as you must repress the sigh of pleasure. In this way, we may achieve that supreme moment in which we die as one."

Oh, had I but known what her use of that term presaged. But I imagined only that she referred to the "little death," as the sensualists of some nations christen that moment when desire expends itself in orgasm and exhaustion.

"Yes! Yes, I understand you, Gamiani!" said Fanny. "Let us begin!"

Placing herself on her back, she opened her legs and held out her arms. "Is this right?"

Seeing the huge machine in Gamiani's hands roused her to even greater lust.

"Or . . . wait. Would you rather have me like this?"

Rolling over, she raised her delectable rump, spread her thighs and, to open herself even more greedily to penetration, reached both hands behind her to spread her vaginal lips.

The sight ravished Gamiani. "Depraved girl! You out do me. How lovely you are, exposed that way."

"Begin, begin, for God's sake!"

But Gamiani, true to her philosophy of restraint and frustration, would not be hurried.

"Oh, but let's prolong this agonizing waiting. Let yourself drift. . . ."

Obediently, Fanny permitted her arms to fall back at her sides, her body to slump, unresponsive, to the sheets.

"It's as if I were already unconscious," whispered Fanny. "I'm dreaming of you now. I belong to you—come. . . ."

"Ah, good, excellent! That's just how I want you."

Passing her hands over Fanny's pale flesh, she murmured, "One would say she was dead. A figure of marble, or wax."

Lying beside her, she whispered in her ear, "I'm going to lay hands upon you, I'll warm you, bring you back to life little by little. I'm going to set you afire, raise you to the uppermost heights of sensual existence. You'll fall back dead again, but dead from pleasure at its most extreme. Unheard of delights! Merely to taste them for the space of two lightning flashes would be the joy of God Almighty!"

Again those references to death. And yet I still, fascinated and excited by the sights displayed before me, failed to grasp her manic and nihilistic purpose.

Knotting up her floating hair as if in in preparation for some gigantic effort, Gamiani slid one hand between her thighs and spent a moment arousing herself.

Thus flushed and humid, she turned to her prey. Her fingers played capriciously in Fanny's hair, which she studied with an indescribable smile of languor and voluptuousness, before throwing herself on Fanny as a lioness on her helpless prey. Her lips forced that vermilion mouth to open, her tongue pumped pleasure from it. Kisses, tender nips flew everywhere, touched her in every place, from head to foot—literally, since she tickled those feet with her fingertips and tongue.

She hurled herself bodily at Fanny, drew away, repeated the breathless, outrageous attack. It was as if she possessed a multitude of heads, of hands. Fanny was kissed, licked, rubbed, handled, stroked in every way. She was pinched, squeezed, bitten. Once, the girl's courage wavered, and she let out a shrill scream; but a delicate touch immediately assuaged her pain and drew from her a long answering sigh.

More ardent, in greater haste, Gamiani parted her victim's thighs. Her fingers toyed with coral lips, abused them, maltreating and tearing the sensitive flesh. Her tongue drove into the flower's calix. Keeping a close watch upon the progress of the delirium she was causing, she stopped, slowed, or quickened her activity according to the approach or retreat of pleasure's ultimate spasm.

Thus did my dear Fanny know all the delights, all the most incendiary sensations a woman is able to experience, and, at last, with a spasm as extreme as a seizure, came with a furious explosion.

"It is too much," cried my darling. "Oh! I am slain!"

To see these two nude, immobile women, welded, as it were, together, one might have imagined a mysterious fusion had taken place, that their souls were conjoining in silence.

Gamiani, bending close to Fanny's mouth, drank in her breath, while her hand, reaching to a low side table by the bed, returned with a vial. Unstopping it, she drank half the contents, then raised Fanny's head and put it to her lips.

"Drink! It is the elixir of life! Your powers will come back! Swallow it."

Annihilated, incapable of resistance, Fanny let Gamiani pour the liquid into her half-open mouth.

As she did so, a single word was expelled from Gamiani's lips. A triumphant but horrible syllable.

"Mine!"

Kneeling between Fanny's legs, she tightened the straps that fastened the formidable device around her slim loins. Upon beholding it, Fanny's transports doubled in violence. It seemed as if an inner fire were tormenting her and flinging her into rage. Spreading her thighs to their limits, she raised her hips to meet the monstrous instrument.

How little she knew of what was to come. Scarcely had the metal shaft begun inexorably to enter her than she fell back to the bed, in the grip of a convulsion.

"Something is burning me! Oh, my bowels, my stomach! But it stings! It tears."

She caught Gamiani's eyes, and in them grasped the terrible truth.

"Oh, I am going to die. Vile bitch, damned sorceress!"

Heedless of these anguished, tortured screams, Gamiani thrust the dildo deeper, reducing to a ruin that part of Fanny's body which had formerly given her such pleasure. And she did so, her own eyes began to roll in their sockets. Her limbs spasmed.

No longer doubting that what she had drunk herself and administered to Fanny was not an aphrodisiac but a deadly poison, I rushed from my hiding place and burst into their chamber.

I reached the bed—but too late! Fanny was dead. Her legs, her arms, hideously contorted, were linked with those of Gamiani, who, alone of the two, still battled with death.

For all her sins and the vileness she had perpetrated, I still retained some shred of the attraction that had drawn me to this doomed woman. And, as she still lived, perhaps she might yet be saved.

But when I attempted to separate her from the corpse of her victim, she resisted with the last of her energy.

"Get out!" she said in a throaty, dying voice. "This woman is mine!"

"Can you be so . . . hideous?" I cried, reeling from the horror. "Even in death . . . ?"

"Ah, you realize it then, sweet fool! I, who have known every sensual extravagance, wished to discover whether in poison's death-grip . . . in this girl's last agony confounded with my own . . . there might not be a possibility . . . a possibility of pleasure . . . the extreme of pleasure in the extreme of pain . . ."

She seemed transfigured by some monstrous revelation, but I was never to know what truth her experiment had revealed.

"No more," she cried. "I . . . no more . . . oh . . ."

And with a long-drawn cry from the depth of her breast, the demoness fell back dead upon the body of the beautiful girl she had killed.

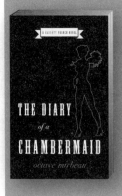